# BY THE HANDS OF
# PARTIES UNKNOWN

# BY THE HANDS OF
# PARTIES UNKNOWN

Gregory S. Sweatt

RESOURCE *Publications* · Eugene, Oregon

BY THE HANDS OF PARTIES UNKNOWN

Resource Publications
An Imprint of Wipf and Stock Publishers
199 W. 8th Ave., Suite 3
Eugene, OR 97401

www.wipfandstock.com

PAPERBACK ISBN: 979-8-3852-4560-4
HARDCOVER ISBN: 979-8-3852-4561-1
EBOOK ISBN: 979-8-3852-4562-8

For my sons
Nathan and Stephen
Sweatt,
The Reverend's
great, great, great grandsons

# Contents

# I

# The Reverend

THE OLD MAN ROSE from his chair at the front of the church and slowly made his way to the pulpit. He was a large man—some of the townsfolk described him as portly—and he stood close to six feet in height. His round bald head, now beaded with perspiration, had a fringe of gray hair running from ear to ear. His brogans hadn't seen a shine in months, and his black frock coat, now faded to a deep gray, was frayed at the cuffs and collar. The white cotton shirt he wore was stained a light yellow. He wore a black cravat neatly tied around his neck.

This was the Reverend Nathan Sweatt, Methodist minister and pastor of this, his church. The year was 1863 on a hot Sunday morning, September 1.

As he approached the pulpit he looked over his congregation. This was his flock. Almost all the wooden benches were full, and he knew the names of every person sitting in them. Some were fanning themselves with whatever they could find. The air in the little church was oppressively hot even with the two windows on either side of the hall wide open. This was the usual weather for that time of year in Attala County, Mississippi.

The Reverend smiled as he looked at his wife, Margaret, and their seven children sitting in the first row. Seven, yes. But it should have been nine. He missed his two sons, William Thomas and

1

Nathan Nawls, dearly. He knew they were safe where they were, out of reach from Confederate authorities. He wished it hadn't been necessary, but at least they were out of harm's way.

The hymn *Nearer, My God, to Thee* still echoed off the rafters as the congregants took their seats. Nathan Sweatt grabbed each side of the rough hewn wood pulpit, then dabbed his forehead with his handkerchief and began.

"The Lord tells us to love our neighbor." He spoke in a soft gentle way, without anger, as though he were speaking with a friend. "This we read from Matthew 22:37. But is this what our country has been doing for the past three years? In Psalm 46 we are told that God is our refuge and strength, a tested help in times of trouble. And so we need not fear even if the world blows up, and the mountains crumble into the sea. Let the oceans roar and foam, let the mountains tremble." He paused as he dabbed his forehead once again and looked into the faces before him. "We can find peace in our troubled world in the Lord himself."

Nathan Sweatt looked older than his fifty-six years. He was born in South Carolina in 1807 or 1808—no one knew for certain, not even the Reverend himself. He married Margaret Elvina, also from South Carolina, and together, after moving to Georgia, began their family. Margaret was a short spare woman with long black hair, large black eyes, and olive skin. All their children would be born in Georgia except for their two youngest. John and Cicero would be the first born as Mississippi natives.

As Nathan looked at his family, he remembered when he first felt the "calling." He and Margaret had settled on a little plot of land near Oxford, Georgia. They were just beginning their family. One day, after coming in from the fields, he sat down on their porch. It was a warm day, and he was exhausted. He wiped his brow with the sleeve of his shirt and looked at his wife. Margaret had been waiting for him, as usual, with a glass of cold water. Nathan thought for a moment, then took a long swallow of the cool liquid.

"There's got to be more than this, Marg," Nathan said as he took another long sip from the glass. "I feel I need to do more than simply live the life God has given me. There's a call I feel inside me to spread the Lord's word beyond the four walls where we live. I feel it in my head and in my heart, and I can't shake it loose. And I don't want to."

Margaret watched quietly as her husband sipped his water. "What do you want to do?" She knew there was more.

Nathan wiped his brow again and paused before answering. "I'd like to go to Emory and study on this a little more. Study the Scriptures." Emory College was a Methodist Episcopal school founded in 1836. The town of Oxford, just west of Atlanta, grew up around the college. "I'd like to get myself on firm ground so I can better say to others what I feel myself. I can farm, I can work the soil, but I can do so much more. I know I can. Do you think this is foolish?" He placed his glass on the porch and turned to look at her.

Margaret rubbed her hands together, then took his hands in hers. "If this is your calling, if this is something you need to do, then follow it."

"It won't be easy, Marg. We have a farm and young ones to consider."

"Nathan, we will get by. If you want to aim for Emory College, then aim true and do what you have to do." She smiled at her husband and looked him in the eye. "We'll get by," she said again.

Nathan smiled like a child who had just received an unexpected gift. "I can work the farm in the morning, do my schooling in the afternoons, and study my theology at night," he said eagerly. "It'll be a tough road, but I think I can do it. I need to do it." Nathan Sweatt was young enough and strong enough for the task he set for himself. His faith would carry him. This he knew.

He then gave his wife a sad look when he said, "It's terrible, Margaret, what people do to their fellow man, to God's children. Yesterday I saw a wagon full of slaves on its way to Atlanta. Those people were dressed in rags and chained together. The children, too. It's not right, and it made me sick."

In time his task, like his family, grew. The hours and the labor were difficult, but the task and his goal never changed. As his studies neared completion, Nathan saw that his task was all but over, too. He knew what came next.

Even though Nathan was a farmer, he knew his prospects in Georgia were slim. The red clay soil was poor, the ground hard, and the rainfall sparse. In 1848 he decided to pull up stakes and bring his family to Mississippi. They settled in Attala County, where the soil was rich, the sun hot, and the water plentiful. When people would ask why they chose Attala to make their home, Nathan would always answer, with a twinkle in his eye, "That's where the wagon broke down."

The entire population of Attala County was only a little over 4,000 in 1840, and that included whites, slaves, freedmen, and Indians. Although farming was the primary county industry, Attala and Kosciusko, the county seat, also supported a blacksmith, woodworkers, and a gist and sawmill.

The Reverend farmed what he could—mostly hay, wheat, some corn and sweet potatoes—on his few acres of land behind his little house in the area of Liberty Chapel, a tiny hamlet northeast of Kosciusko. Nathan would load his wagon with what he could, and, with the help of James his young son, ride the few miles into Kosciusko to sell his produce at the local dry goods store, then pick up whatever provisions his family might need and return home. Nathan Sweatt became a familiar face in Kosciusko. His gentle nature and quiet demeanor made him many friends.

It was there in Attala that Nathan Sweatt began his ministry. It started small, with his neighbors in both Liberty Chapel and Kosciusko. They would discuss their faith, their families, their hopes and dreams, and sometimes even a little politics. The Reverend would listen quietly and offer suggestions, answers, and possibilities when asked. At times he would offer condolences to those in grief. Over the years his ministry gained a nice following. His small clapboard church, built with the help of many parishioners, stood not far from his home. Sundays saw the little meeting house full at every service. Nathan and his family, all dressed in their finest, were the first to arrive and the last to leave.

4

Storm clouds of war, though, were forming over the nation in 1860. The Reverend could see them coming, and when Mississippi seceded from the country he loved Nathan knew what he had to do. The Confederate States of America began drafting young men for military service on April 16, 1862. The Reverend would not wait that long.

Gathering his family together around the parlor hearth one night Nathan told Margaret and the children what must be done. The parlor was dark, the only light coming from the small fire burning before them. It cast a soft yellow glow on their faces. Their daughters Easter, Margaret, Mary, and Amanda sat alongside their sons James, John, and Cicero. Their oldest sons, William and Nathan, sat quietly nearby.

William, the older of the two boys, was a good two inches taller than his father. He had a slender, but muscular build. His head was topped with a thatch of dark brown hair. His eyes betrayed a mind deep in thought. William always chose his words carefully before speaking, and his voice, like the Reverend's, had a soft tone to it. His brother, Nathan, was a bit shorter than William. Nate's hair and bushy eyebrows framed a square face and chin. He had the dark penetrating eyes of his mother. Like his brother, Nathan also had a strong muscular body, the result of years of hard farm work and manual labor.

"William and Nathan need to go," he said in a low voice. Margaret's face dropped. She knew he was right. She and her husband had discussed this among themselves, but the reality was now in front of her.

"Where, Nathan?" she whispered.

"I'm figuring Indian Territory, west of here. They'll be safe there. We'll give them a goodly amount of supplies, as best we can at least, to get 'em started on their way. I leave it up to them where to settle. The boys are old enough and big enough to fend for themselves. They'll be safe there," he said again, more to reassure himself than anyone else. William Thomas and Nathan Nawls were in their 20's. He only hoped he was right. The children sat silent. Some of the younger ones began to cry. The two oldest boys sat staring at the fire.

Margaret looked Nathan squarely in the eyes. "Are you sure?" she said in a steady voice.

"You know my feelings on this, Margaret. I abhor violence. I abhor it for my family. I abhor it for my country. And that's where we're headed." He stared into the fire. Almost more to himself than his family, he said, "My sons, our sons, will not lift arms against their fellow man. We both know this. William and Nate know this. It's not a matter of being scared. It's a matter of right against wrong." He turned back to look at his wife.

"They'll be comin' for 'em, Marg, you know they will. The authorities are going to sweep up any boy they can lay their hands on and toss 'em into the army. I'll be damned if Bill and Nate will be two of 'em."

William turned from the fire and looked at his mother. "We'll be fine, Ma. We will. Me an' Nate can take care of ourselves. We can work the land, hunt if we have to, or even hire ourselves out to another farmer if need be. Won't be long before we get our feet under us and start anew." Margaret took both their hands in hers and simply nodded her head.

Later that night, as William and Nathan lay awake in their beds, the only sounds they heard came from the night crickets singing their usual song. The rest of the house was quiet.

In a whisper Nathan asked his brother, "You scared, Bill?"

There was a long pause before William answered. "Sure I am, Nate. I'm guessin' you are, too, no matter what Pa says." William thought for a second. "But he's right. We gotta leave here 'less you want to be a soldier. There's gonna be a war for sure, and I won't stand for no killin'. Pa an' Ma raised us right as far as I see it. An' slavery? That don't sit with me any more'n killin' does."

"I'm scared for certain," whispered Nathan. "Don't know what to expect wherever we go, but for certain I don't see me killin' someone. Don't see how God would allow it. Most I ever done was shoot a turkey. But playin' soldier? That ain't for me, neither."

The boys slept in a loft above the parlor. William stared into the darkness. He could barely make out the rafters above his head as the moonlight, dancing between drifting clouds, filtered in and out of the loft's tiny window.

Nathan said softly, "Bill? Think we might sneak back to Attala once in a while to see the family?"

William wouldn't answer directly. He only said, "We'll do all right, Nate. Long as we have each other an' stick together we'll do fine."

It was 1861 when William Thomas and Nathan Nawls set off for the Territory. They left a huge and unknown hole in the Reverend's family. He would never see his boys again.

The Reverend was never one to push his views on others. Nor would he use his pulpit to gather other people to his cause. But the Reverend Nathan Sweatt was a Union man, a northern sympathizer some would say. Even Attala County and Kosciusko had been lukewarm on the subject of secession. His sermon today, though, the one he was giving to his flock, would not be a fire and brimstone speech. He would not inflame his congregation. They knew where he stood on the Confederacy, on slavery, on the war.

Nathan continued, "In Isaiah 42:13 we read, 'The Lord will be a mighty warrior, and full of fury toward his foes. He will give a great shout and prevail. Long has he been silent; he has restrained himself. But now he will give full vent to his wrath; he will groan and cry like a woman delivering her child. He will level the mountains and hills and blight their greenery. He will dry up the rivers and pools. He will bring blind Israel along a path they have not seen before. He will make the darkness bright before them and smooth and straighten out the road ahead. He will not forsake them. But those who trust in idols and call them gods will be greatly disappointed; they will be turned away.'" The Reverend paused, looking at the faces before him. These were his friends, his neighbors. He knew what was in their hearts as much as they knew what was in his.

"My friends, 'The Lord has magnified his law and made it truly glorious. Through it he had planned to show the world that he is righteous. But what a sight his people are—those who were to demonstrate to all the world the glory of his law; for they are robbed, enslaved, imprisoned, trapped, fair game for all, with no one to protect them. Won't one of you apply these lessons from the past and see the ruin that awaits you up ahead?'" Nathan took his handkerchief and dabbed his forehead. He looked again at every face in his congregation before continuing. "I leave it up to each and every one of you to look into your heart. We all know what is right—what God wants us to do—to treat our fellow man the way we ourselves would want to be treated."

Then the Reverend Sweatt, without mentioning the President's name, dared to quote from Lincoln's 1858 speech. "As I would not be a slave, so would I not be a master." He paused once more. "Again, from Isaiah 42, 'That is why God poured out such fury and wrath on his people and destroyed them in battle.'" The entire church was silent. Even those who had been fanning themselves stopped their rustling sound. "And finally, 'Yet, though set on fire and burned, they will not understand the reason why—that it is God, wanting them to repent.'"

Nathan ended his sermon, the closest he would come to using a bully pulpit, by quoting Isaiah 2:4. "And he shall judge among the nations and shall rebuke many people: and they shall beat their swords into plowshares, and their spears into pruning hooks: nation shall not lift up sword against nation, neither shall they learn war anymore."

Reverend Sweatt then raised his arms, as though he were embracing his flock. "Go now in peace and love. And may the Lord be with you always."

As the congregation stood to sing *Amazing Grace*, two soldiers at the back of the church also stood and immediately left. One, a scruffy looking sergeant with faded stripes on his butternut shell jacket, looked as though he hadn't bathed in a month. The other man, a tad bit shorter than the sergeant and just as dirty looking, wore a ragged gray coat and torn brown pants which hardly resembled a uniform at all. Neither man removed his hat during the entire service. The Reverend saw them leave. He knew what to expect. He didn't care.

# 2

# The Captain

WHEN SERGEANT DUNCAN TURNER and Corporal Jimmy Dolan left the Reverend's church they headed straight back to Kosciusko. Their shoes kicked up small clouds of dust as they hurried along the dirt road. The sun beat down on their heads unmercifully.

"Where's Massey?" Dolan asked. His boyish face and curly black hair belied his twenty years.

"Same place as always," replied the sergeant. Turner looked older than his twenty-two years. The deep creases in his face told of a hard life.

"Whatd'ya 'spose he'll do, Dunc?"

"Guess we'll find out," said Turner, as the two soldiers, lacking mounts, made their way back to town on foot. Both men had enlisted in the 20th Mississippi back in '61. They both hailed from Noxubee County, east of Attala.

When they arrived in Kosciusko Turner and Dolan crossed the town square. Dolan looked up at the courthouse, a two story brick building topped with a small white cupola. It was built in 1837. Dolan knew its courtroom was now used as a guardhouse. Like many small country towns, Kosciusko was built around its courthouse. The town square, ringed with wooden sidewalks, held stores, a post office, a hotel, newspaper office, and, of course, a saloon.

Both men were out of breath and sweating profusely by the time they reached their destination. The day was still hot. It had been a long walk, but they had finally arrived at Davis's Tavern. It may have been Sunday, but Jonah Davis was going to keep his saloon open.

The tavern was a dark and dank establishment which smelled of stale tobacco smoke and spilled liquor. It held one small table and two wooden chairs. The bar, a long wood plank supported by two wooden barrels, stood along one wall. A tarnished brass cuspidor rested on the floor near one of the barrels. The cuspidor and the floor around it were covered in black tobacco juice. The small saloon was lit by two candles on each end of the bar. Sergeant Turner and Corporal Dolan stood in the doorway. Massey and Davis were the only two in the tavern. And C.K. Massey was in a black mood.

Conrad K. Massey was captain of Company D, 20th Regiment Mississippi Volunteer Infantry, and as he contemplated his glass of rye he wondered why in hell he was here. While the rest of the 20th was somewhere off in Tennessee or Georgia with the Confederate Army of Tennessee doing some real fighting, he was stuck in this shithole of a town. His orders were to round up any army deserters, stragglers, bushwackers, draft evaders, and Union sympathizers within the county's borders.

He took a sip of the strong amber liquid, then rolled the glass between his fingers. There were other companies raised from Attala County, including Company K from the 20th. Why wasn't Captain Patterson's men here? Why, Massey thought, did I draw this duty? The war had bypassed Attala County for the most part. There were no harbors, railroads, or factories to destroy, so Yankee armies, by and large, left the county alone.

C.K. Massey had high hopes when he joined the 20th back in the late summer of 1861. The regiment was recruited from volunteers in seven Mississippi counties. Attala was not one of them. Massey enlisted in Noxubee County as a private, but was quickly elected captain of Company D. Many companies elected their officers this way. This assignment, though, was not what he expected.

This damn county, he knew, was filled with more deserters than he could ever expect to arrest. These bushwackers and deserters were hiding out in the woods and swamps of every corner of Attala. They knew the land well. Massey had even heard reports from runaway blacks that there was no room for them in the woods because the woods were full of runaway white men.

As post commander in Kosciusko, Massey asked himself, how am I supposed to do this? Regimental command had given him a small detachment of cavalry as a supplement to his infantry, but this was hardly a help. They were undisciplined and had proven to be as big a detriment to the civilian population as the bushwackers themselves, roaming the countryside at will and seizing horses, mules and food. Anything they could lay their hands on. Contraband, as they called it. The cavalry had a poor record of rounding up these deserters, evaders, and Union loyalists anyway, even with the help of a pack of hounds which were used at times. Every patrol returning to town reported to Massey that these bands of bushwackers had eluded them once again. Sometimes the patrols even came under gunfire. And the town wasn't safe either. Massey had learned that a Texas cavalry lieutenant had been shot and killed right here in this tavern back in June.

Massey swallowed the remainder of his drink, then slammed the glass down on the bar. To make matters worse, he thought to himself, the Confederate armies were losing ground everywhere. Corinth had fallen. So had the capital at Jackson. Port Gibson was in Union hands, Champion Hill had been lost, and Vicksburg, damn it all, had surrendered on July 4. Then there was Robert E. Lee who had lost a huge battle up in Pennsylvania. As if that weren't enough Union Colonel Benjamin Grierson had led a cavalry raid through the heart of Mississippi from the Tennessee border to Baton Rouge, Louisiana. Hell, he even heard rumors of unrest in Jones County south of Jackson.

He looked over at Jonah Davis standing behind the bar. "Gimme another," Massey said. Davis just stared at him.

"Not 'til ya pay for what'cha got," Davis snapped back.

Massey reached in his pocket and pulled out a fifty cent Confederate shinplaster, a worthless piece of fractional paper currency, and tossed it on the counter.

"I only take U.S.," snarled Davis. Jonah Davis was a short wiry man with a thin black moustache and black greasy hair.

"Well, Davis, you sure as hell had no problem takin' my money before."

"You paid last time with U.S.," replied Jonah. Massey's last couple of gold pieces had been spent on cigars and rye a week ago.

Massey looked him straight in the eye and said, "I could arrest you, shut this place down, and confiscate all the liquor you have. How's that for payment?"

Davis hesitated, let out a sigh, and pocketed the shinplaster. He filled Massey's glass again, however he kept the bottle of whiskey behind the counter and out of reach of the captain's hands.

Captain Massey didn't suffer fools easily. He had a job to do, whether he liked it or not, and damnit he was going to do it. The captain was a tall, muscular man. He wore a neatly trimmed moustache and goatee, though brown stubble now appeared across his face. His mop of brown hair fell to his ear tops. He wore a gray Confederate frock coat with the three gold bars on his faded blue collar signifying his rank. His uniform's brass buttons were tarnished from years of duty. His gray kepi sat on the bartop. Massey no longer wore an officer's sword. Those things were a nuisance anyway, he remembered. You couldn't walk three feet without the damn thing tangling up your legs. He did carry, however, a Model 1860 Army Colt revolver as a side arm on his sword belt. God, he thought, if only my uniform's authority was enough to do my bidding.

Massey heard a voice behind him.

"Cap'n sir?" It was Duncan.

Massey downed his drink with one swallow, and without turning around said, "Report, Sergeant."

Sergeant Turner and Corporal Dolan, still standing in the doorway, eyed the array of bottles behind the bar. The day was still warm, their walk had been long, and their throats dry.

"He's at agin, Cap'n. He's givin' all that Yankee talk to his church folk," Turner said with a scratchy voice. "He's talkin' 'bout swords an' spears an' hooks an' all. He said the world's gonna blow up, or somethin' like that." This was patently false, and the sergeant knew it.

"Well, Sergeant, you certainly know your Scripture," Massey said with a hint of sarcasm. "Thank you. I'll take it from here. You're dismissed."

Massey walked out of the tavern without giving Jonah Davis or the two soldiers a second look. He headed straight towards the courthouse. The streets of Kosciusko were all but deserted.

# 3

# The Conversation

CAPTAIN MASSEY SAT IN a small office on the ground floor of the courthouse. He had commandeered the office as his headquarters. It adjoined the courtroom, which now served as a jail, and had been the Chancery Clerk's office. Massey had no idea where the clerk, James Wallace, had relocated. He was gone. That was all that mattered. Massey's sword belt hung from a peg on the wall. His coat was draped over the back of his chair. He pulled his suspenders, commonly called braces, off his shoulders and let them fall to his sides. Then he settled himself into his chair.

It had been several days since he had received Sergeant Turner's report on the Reverend Sweatt's Sunday sermon. As Massey sat sucking on a cigar, filling his office with white smoke, he reviewed in his mind the events just past.

The more than worthless cavalry patrols had been returning to his headquarters empty-handed. Once, however, they did scoop up and return to the courthouse an old man, well into his 70's Massey guessed, who Logan Burke, the captain in charge of the cavalry, insisted was an army deserter. Captain Massey, exasperated once again, told Burke to return the old man to his home, somewhere around Possumneck near the Big Black River. The horse patrols were giving Massey nothing, but he would send them out again anyway. Maybe next time he thought.

Massey took a few good puffs on his cigar and told himself that maybe it was time to have another talk with the good Reverend. He had spoken with Nathan Sweatt on more than one occasion, usually when the Reverend came to town on his regular visits. Massey would press the Reverend on his loyalties, his movements within the county, and, especially, the whereabouts of his two sons, both of whom had been missing since the beginning of the war. They should be in the army, Massey knew, and he wanted to find out where they were. The army needed men now more than ever.

Everyone in town knew of the Reverend's Union leanings, including Captain Massey. Everyone also knew the Reverend was a respected member of the community. So did Massey. This next conversation with Nathan Sweatt would have to be handled carefully, just as the others had been.

Massey got up from his chair and pulled on his uniform coat, wrapped his officer's belt around his waist and clicked the buckle, then walked outside looking for Burke. He didn't have to look far. The captain was leaning against a hitching post and smoking a cheroot. When he saw Massey, Burke immediately stood and faced him. He still held the small cigar. He wasn't going to lose his last one.

"Captain, send the patrol out again. See what you can find." It was still morning, and Massey knew the horse soldiers could cover a lot of ground while daylight lasted. "Take the dogs if you wish."

"Yes sir," answered Burke while giving a sloppy salute to the captain. Massey returned the salute with a halfhearted one of his own as Captain Burke walked to the stables where the cavalry mounts were quartered. Burke and Massey both held the rank of captain. Burke, though, was junior to Massey in both age and date of promotion. Logan Burke, much to his displeasure, was subject to Massey's orders. This did not sit well with him.

Captain Massey remembered when Reverend Sweatt made his usual trips into Kosciusko. He could almost set his pocket watch by it. Today was one of those days, and he knew where the Reverend would be.

Massey walked over to the town's grocery and dry goods store. It sat on the far side of the square from his office. The sidewalks were bustling with people. He noticed the looks and sideway stares he was getting from the townspeople as he passed them. Were they frightened by him? Suspicious of him? Or just plain angry with him? It didn't really matter. The captain felt that a little apprehension of the military on the town's part wasn't a bad thing.

As he got closer to the store he recognized Reverend Sweatt's wagon. It was tied up out front. There appeared to be some activity around it. The Reverend and his son James were loading the wagon with their usual provisions. Good Lord, Massey thought as he eyed the advertisements in the store's window. This war has driven prices out of hand. A pair of shoes cost $15, and a lady's bonnet $60. A chicken would run a person $15, and a barrel of flour $75. Massey chuckled to himself; that would assume a person could even find those items. As he approached the wagon Massey wondered how the Reverend's family could pay for what they bought.

Nathan Sweatt had been doing business at Henderson's Grocery almost as long as he and his family had lived in Attala County. Nathan and John Henderson had become good friends over the years. The Reverend's trips into town gave him the opportunity to not only conduct business at the little store, but also to talk to Henderson about the war, the county, the state, and the nation. Nathan always made sure to ask about Henderson's family whenever he was in town.

When the Reverend sold his produce at Henderson's store he was always paid in U.S. currency. But as the war continued, and Mississippi's economy deteriorated, this became more difficult. Soon Nathan was forced to accept Confederate currency and notes. These were backed at the capitol in Richmond by practically nothing. They were all but worthless, and inflation was running rampant throughout the state and the South. In time the Reverend and John Henderson were forced to devise a barter system. This worked more as a necessity than a solution. It wasn't perfect but it worked for the two men, and neither felt he was being cheated by the other.

Nathan and James had just delivered baskets of corn, sweet potatoes, peas, a few eggs, and two live chickens. In exchange John Henderson had offered grain, some cloth, molasses, a new hoe, and a half pound of sugar, an item worth its weight in gold in 1863. The Reverend had stopped on his way out the door. It was a warm day, and Nathan patted his forehead with his handkerchief.

"A pleasure as always, John. See you and Ruth Sunday?"

John Henderson gripped the Reverend's hand and smiled. "You'll see us there, Nate."

Nathan looked out the shop's door and saw Captain Massey standing next to his wagon. He let a wary look cross his face. Henderson noticed Massey also and sighed. "More of the same?"

"Looks like it, John. Not to worry, though. This'll be another tussle, I'm sure." Nathan wanted to change the subject. Anything to do with the captain was always distasteful. "Say, John, how long you think we can keep this Injun trading going?" The Reverend gave Henderson a wink and a grin.

"Heck, I don't know, Nate. Maybe 'til were both pushin' up daisies." He put his hand on Nathan's shoulder. "Be strong," he said softly.

"Strong? That's my middle name, John, don'tcha know?"

Henderson looked at the Reverend with a furrowed expression. "How long d'ya think this can go on, Nate?" Henderson practically whispered this.

Nathan knew exactly what the storekeeper meant. They had had many discussions on this very subject over the months and years. Quietly he said, "Can't see it going on much longer, John. Leastwise not here in Mississippi. The state's all but under Union control. Attala seems to be more menaced by bandits than any Federal soldiers. Rumor has it that Confederate armies are backing off on almost all fronts. Spilled blood everywhere. And for what?" Nathan wouldn't venture any further.

John Henderson knew Nathan's sentiments on these matters. And although he agreed with the Reverend, he would only speak in hushed tones. There were several other customers in his shop, and not knowing their opinions on the war and slavery he said to Nathan in a low voice, "It's gotta stop, Nate. When all's said an' done it'll be years before the county will be able to get back on its feet. I'm with you, there. What a terrible waste."

Nathan gave Henderson a knowing look and simply nodded his head. He hoisted the grain on his shoulder and headed out the door.

Massey was waiting and wasted no time. "A word with you Reverend, if I could?" Massey was trying to be cordial.

Here we go again, thought Nathan. "As you wish, Captain." He dropped the sack of grain into the bed of the wagon and turned to face James. "Son, run inside and get that bolt of cloth your mother's been wanting. And don't forget the jar of molasses."

"Doin' pretty well I see," said Massey. "How d'ya do it?"

He's fishing, thought Nathan. And it's none of his business anyway. "We get by."

"Got a lot of mouths to feed. Must be tough."

"Well, Captain, I don't suppose you're here to ask about the well being of my family," replied Nathan in a quiet voice. "Why don't you just get to the point." The Reverend knew what this was all about. He'd been through it before.

Massey shifted a little, looking down at the ground. He kicked a little pebble away with the toe of his boot. "I don't think it's any secret you're a Union man. The whole town knows it. The whole county knows it. You're an abolitionist, ain't ya?"

"Do I think a man should own another man? No, I don't. If that makes me an abolitionist then so be it," Nathan said in a calm voice. "I don't own any slaves." He had witnessed a slave auction in Georgia. He saw humans chained, sold, and carted away. He had seen it in Alabama and Mississippi; families torn apart, brutality inflicted. It made him sick.

"You're in the Confederacy, Reverend. This is our country."

"My country is the United States. It's yours, too."

Massey was getting irritated. "You're spillin' your ideas onto a lot of folks. We don't need your type of trouble. We don't need…"

Nathan interrupted, "I have never asked anyone to believe what I believe." He left it at that.

Massey was now angry. This was not going well. He blurted out, "Where are your two sons?"

"I don't know," Nathan said simply. It was the truth. Two years ago William Thomas and Nathan Nawls had left for the Indian Territory. They could be anywhere by now. He hadn't heard from them at all. Did they stay there? Did they move on? He had no idea.

"Well, Reverend, I just don't think that's the whole truth. Your boys are of draft age and should be in the army. Now why don'tcha just tell me where they are." Massey was almost shouting. He glared at the Reverend.

"I don't know," replied Nathan again, his voice low and even.

"Sure would be a shame if somethin' were to happen to your family, say, or your home or church."

"Are you threatening me, Captain?" Nathan asked.

"There's a lot of loyal Southerners around here. Loyal to the Confederacy, that is. You're sorta outnumbered I'd reckon." Massey was playing all his cards. He had never gone this far, maybe too far. Nathan said nothing.

"Where are they?" Massey yelled. His face was bright red. He knew this was pointless.

"Are we finished, Captain?" James was walking out of the dry goods store carrying the molasses and an armful of cloth, followed by John Henderson.

"There a problem here?" asked Henderson. John Henderson was an imposing sight. Standing at a good six feet, four inches and weighing close to two hundred twenty pounds, he towered over Captain Massey. He had a bushy black mustache and thick black hair. His voice was as deep as a bear's growl.

Massey looked at the boy, at Henderson, then back at the Reverend. By now a small crowd had gathered wondering what the commotion was all about. He turned on his heels and stormed off. This was not what he intended at all. But there was another small piece of business he needed to take care of.

Massey strode over to the office of the Kosciusko *Chronicle*, ignoring the stares he received from everyone he passed. The outside wall of the office had issues of the *Chronicle* pinned across it with the latest town news. He entered the office and slammed the door behind him. The office walls were covered with notes, clippings, handwritten sheets of paper, and old issues of the newspaper. George Harlow, the paper's editor, stood next to his press. He waved an ink covered hand at Massey.

"Howdy, Captain. What can I do for ya?" Harlow was a tall thin man with a bald head and white whiskers. He wore small wire rimmed spectacles. An ink smeared apron covered his chest. The entire office smelled of printer's ink.

"I read a letter you printed the other day. It was abolitionist through and through. I want to know who wrote it." The *Chronicle* was a Whig paper and anti-slavery in its editorial point of view.

Harlow had worked as an apprentice at the *Chronicle* as a young man. For years he learned the newspaper trade from bottom to top. As a boy he would sweep the office, clean the press, distribute the papers around town, and gather the latest news, gossip, and business dealings, bringing it all back to his boss for the next *Chronicle* edition. All this while going to school, continuing his education, and reading as many books as he could lay his hands on.

George Harlow never embraced secession, and thought the country was heading down a dark road because of it. He always tried to be fair in his reporting but refused to outright lie in his accounts of battles, information coming from Richmond, or news from the North if he could at all help it. This, of course, put him at odds with C.K. Massey when it came to news that put the Confederacy in a poor light. When Harlow reprinted an article from the *Abington Virginian* newspaper back in July which announced a huge Confederate victory at Gettysburg, he immediately retracted it when he learned the complete opposite was true, going so far as to reprint an article he had obtained from the *Columbia and Bloomsburg General Advertiser*, up North, which told an entirely different, and subsequently true, account. Irritating Captain Massey even further were the factual accounts Harlow printed covering the fall of Jackson, Vicksburg, and the Confederate defeat at Champion Hill.

In time Harlow's sentiments about the war, the Confederacy, and slavery brought him into the confidences and friendship of the Reverend Nathan Sweatt. During his many trips into Kosciusko Nathan would oftentimes drop by the *Chronicle* office, sit by the stove, and spend time in conversation with the editor. Their similar views on the South and its deteriorating condition due to the war formed a bond between the two men which withstood the outside pressures created by Massey's occupation of the town. George Harlow and Nathan Sweatt were in lockstep when it came to where the South was headed, and why it was heading there.

"I know the piece yer talkin' 'bout," said Harlow, as he wiped his glasses with a clean rag. "Can't help ya there, Captain. Sorry" The letter had been signed 'Concerned Citizen.'

"Not good enough, Harlow," said Massey, the irritation still in his voice. Harlow was a little too chipper for the captain's mood.

"Captain, the letter in question was dropped off here by someone fer sure. Thing is, I don't know by who. It was slipped under my office door." The letter itself was certainly inflammatory. In so many words it condemned slavery, criticized the war, praised President Lincoln, and put the blame for the poor state of affairs in the South squarely on the shoulders of Jefferson Davis and the Confederacy.

Massey, still upset, said, "So you just print anything anyone gives you?"

"That's 'bout the nature of it. I even print t'other side, too. Why don'tcha write something up yerself, Captain. I'd run it."

Massey began walking through the office looking at the walls plastered with old newspapers and notes. He looked at the racks filled with metal type and the single press Harlow leaned against. Turning to face the editor Massey said, "You're friendly with the Reverend Sweatt, ain't ya? Know him pretty good, do ya?"

Harlow chuckled a little. "Yes sir. I know Nate. I know a lot of folks in this town. Doc Galloway, John Henderson, Jim Wallace, Mayor Mosby…you." Harlow smiled at the captain. "Would ya like me to introduce ya to any of 'em?" He was playing with Massey now.

"I've seen the Reverend stop by your office, here. You two talk a lot?" Massey tried to keep his voice under control.

"Sure. We talk. Spin a few tales, pass the time." Harlow paused, then added, "Sometimes we talk the Bible, sometimes politics, sometimes the war." The editor paused again, then said, "What we say is 'tween him and me."

Ignoring what Harlow had just told him, Massey said, "Has he ever told you where his sons are?"

George Harlow couldn't resist. "Why come to think of it he has. I do believe he said his sons are on his farm with his wife an' daughters."

Massey began to boil. "I'm not talkin' 'bout them! Did he tell you where his oldest boys are?"

"Nope, never did," Harlow calmly replied. He enjoyed seeing the captain flummoxed.

"So yer sayin' that in all these talks you an' the pastor had, he never said nothin' 'bout the whereabouts of his boys?"

"Never. Ain't none a my business, neither."

"Well, it's my business," Massey yelled.

George Harlow looked Captain Massey square in the eyes. "Why don'tcha leave it be? Nate's a peace lovin' man, a good man, a God fearin' family man. He don't cause trouble. If he says he don't know where his boys are at, it's the truth. Nate don't lie."

"And I 'spose you have no idea if that letter was writ by the Reverend?" Massey wouldn't let it go.

"Like I told ya. Can't help ya there." Harlow had a smug look on his face, and Massey didn't like it.

The captain wasn't satisfied. "It'd be a shame if I had to shut you down." More threats. Seemed like his day was full of them.

"Well, Captain, that ya could do if ya had a mind to. I could do nothin' 'bout it. But the town sure might."

Is he threatening me now? Massey wondered. I better count my losses and leave, he said to himself. He took a last look around the office, fixed his eyes on Harlow and the press, and left.

In a matter of days he had laid threats at the feet of three people, and might have received one of his own.

Massey headed straight for the tavern.

# 4

# The Ambush

THE NEXT MORNING, SEPTEMBER 6, Captain Massey wanted to send the cavalry out earlier than usual. He wanted the horsemen to sweep north of Kosciusko. Massey had heard reports from some of the townsfolk that there were groups of deserters hiding in the woods near Liberty Chapel. Pretty near the Reverend's farm, Massey thought. He wondered if there was a connection.

"Sergeant Turner!" Massey yelled.

Turner, standing right outside Massey's office, quickly walked in. "Sir?"

"Track down Captain Burke. Tell him to see me at once." Sergeant Turner left in search of Burke not knowing where to find him.

The cavalry detachment had set up its camp just beyond the town proper. Turner figured he'd start there. He hadn't gone fifty yards when he spotted Corporal Dolan over by the blacksmith shop talking to some of the infantry privates. God knows what Jimmy is saying, Turner thought. Probably lording over them the fact that he has corporal stripes and they didn't. "Dolan, come 'ere!" Dolan hurried over. "S'up Sergeant?"

"Follow me. Gotta find Burke. Cap'n wants to find him pretty damn quick," said Turner. Dolan saw they were headed towards the cavalry camp outside of town.

"He ain't there, Dunc. Saw him earlier at the stables."

Shit, Turner said to himself. We'll be walkin' all over town lookin' for that pompous ass.

They found Burke just inside the barn grooming his mount, a sturdy chestnut stallion. Captain Logan Burke was a blonde haired, blue eyed man with a fair complexion and smooth skin. His clean shaven face revealed a square jaw. He had an annoying way of talking to anyone he met in a condescending manner while at the same time looking right through the person. His uniform was immaculate.

Logan Burke, like Conrad Massey, Duncan Turner, and Jimmy Dolan, also hailed from Noxubee County. The three men knew each other but were hardly friends. When Burke enlisted in Company D in October of 1861 Massey had already been elected captain two months earlier. This stuck in Burke's craw. He felt he should be on at least equal footing with Massey.

Burke's skill on horseback, coupled with his authoritative nature and commanding presence, easily got him elected captain, and he was given a small cavalry command. He stood a solid five feet, eight inches tall and, like Massey, had a muscular build. His habit of talking down to everyone in his command made him an elitist in the eyes of his men. He didn't care. Their job was to follow.

Logan Burke admired J.E.B. Stuart. The accomplishments of the dashing general were not lost on him. Neither was Stuart's flamboyant style. The general's two successful cavalry rides around the entire Army of the Potomac in 1862 were already legendary. His dashing nature was the envy of Burke. The captain was well aware of all this, and he was determined to emulate the man. Burke had pulled up one side of his gray felt hat, fastened it, and attached a large black crow's feather to it. He began to wear a cape, trimmed in red, across his shoulders. This, he knew, gave him the image he desired, if only in his own mind. Burke's high opinion of himself was shared by no one else.

"Well, if it isn't our own Sergeant and his little mouse. What can I do for you two?" Turner wasn't intimidated by Burke, his rank nor his attitude. Dolan stood silent looking at nothing in particular.

"Cap'n Massey wants to see you right away."

"I'll be along shortly. That'll be all, Sergeant. Thank you." Burke continued to brush his horse.

Turner and Dolan left, neither caring whether Logan showed up at Massey's office at all. "He'll get his," Turner muttered to himself.

"You wanted to see me, Captain?" Burke found Captain Massey standing outside the courthouse chewing on his cigar.

Massey, with a concerned look on his face, said, "Captain, I want you to send your men out again. Go up towards Liberty Chapel. There's some activity there; reports of camps, movement, squatters, theft. You know the routine."

Burke thought for a second before answering. "That's up near the Reverend's farm. You want me to put a little scare in him?"

"No!" Massey was emphatic. "Leave him alone." Massey's verbal tussle with Nathan Sweatt the day before was enough for now. "Let it lie."

Burke's cavalry patrols were usually eight man squads. Not today, though. "Captain, Wilson and Hart are sick. They say they got the vapors or somethin'. They're layin' low right now. We'll have to go with six," said Burke.

"Then six it is."

"As you wish," replied Burke, as he gave the captain another sloppy salute and made his way back to the cavalry camp.

Logan Burke's cavalry squad was a sight to behold. Their uniforms were a patchwork of Confederate gray, butternut, and civilian. Some of the horsemen even wore sky blue trousers they had taken at one time or another from Yankee prisoners or, at worse, dead Yankees.

Burke, like Massey, carried an army Colt revolver. Unlike Massey, however, Captain Burke did carry a saber. He felt it fit the image he saw of himself as the dashing cavalier. About the only equipment Burke's men carried that was similar was their carbines. They were each armed with a British pattern 1856 muzzle loading, smoothbore carbine. These were clumsy weapons, time consuming to load, and inaccurate at extreme distances. But they were all they had. A few of the horsemen also wore side arms, and one or two carried a cavalry saber.

"Kirkland, Howard, Cox, Morgan, Ford, Douglass!" shouted Burke in an angry voice. "Saddle up now!" The six gathered their horses from the stables, assembled their gear, and reported back to the captain as fast as they could. When the squad was ready to move out Burke turned in his saddle and took a long, weary look at them. What a sad sight, he thought. It'll have to do. "And leave the dogs," he added. "They'll only slow us down."

The sun was still low in the east when the cavalry patrol moved out. The red of dawn slowly gave way to a clear blue sky. The seven horsemen rode northeast out of Kosciusko along the Natchez Trace at a slow trot. This would take them in the direction of Liberty Chapel. As much as Burke wanted to show that abolitionist Reverend a thing or two he followed Massey's orders and gave the Reverend's farm a wide berth.

The day was warming up quickly as the patrol passed the village of Ethel. The small wood and log homes were spread far apart. Captain Burke saw very few people. He thought, if nothing else, they could forage a little along the way; chickens, hogs, corn, cows . . . whatever they could find. Ethel proved fruitless. It had been stripped clean, probably by bushwackers or bandits. Possibly by his own men. The squad turned west.

They were riding in a column of twos through forests of oak, scrub pine, tall grass, and open meadows. Burke looked to his left and right. There could be a man right now, he thought to himself, hiding behind a tree, gun in hand, and putting his sights on any one of us. He took a deep breath. The air was crisp and fresh even in the day's heat. The scent of pine was everywhere. Pine needles and leaves littered the ground in a soft cover. A few trees had their leaves beginning to turn. The sky was cloudless.

In the back of his mind Captain Burke still wanted to roundup the old man Massey ordered returned to Possumneck. Farmer my ass, he thought. He was a deserter plain and simple. Burke didn't care. He was surrounded by renegades and bushwackers, deserters and stragglers. Age didn't matter to him. If they were old enough to carry a gun, they were old enough to aim and fire it.

After covering a few miles the squad came to a ford on the Scoobachita Creek. The creek ran through a small clearing surrounded by pine woods. The Scoobachita was a tiny tributary of the larger Zilpha Creek which ran east to west and flowed into the Big Black River.

Captain Burke ordered a halt. "Dismount. Water up." The horsemen grabbed their canteens and took deep swallows, washing the dust from their throats. The horses bowed their heads into the creek and lapped up the water. No one spoke as the men refilled their canteens from the little stream. A few birds could be heard singing in the distance, otherwise it was quiet.

The first shot, a loud crack, came from behind a tree somewhere in the woods which circled the meadow. At the sound every soldier took a knee. Each held onto the reins of his horse. The animals jumped and tugged upon hearing the shot. It missed but was followed by multiple rounds from hidden guns in the trees. The shots came from everywhere and every angle. The forest exploded with gunfire. One round grazed Cox in the thigh. Morgan and Douglass each received bullets to their arms. Morgan had a chunk of flesh ripped from his left arm, and Douglass had a bullet lodge near his right shoulder. Howard was untouched, as was Ford, but lost his hat when a round tore it from his head. Men were screaming, Burke was shouting. He fired his Colt anywhere he could and at any muzzle flash he saw.

"Return fire, damnit!" His men began to fire their carbines blindly into the woods. There were no targets. "Take cover!" There was no cover to take. The cavalry squad was completely exposed in the meadow. Each time one of Burke's men fired a round he had to stop and muzzle load his weapon again, slamming a charge down the carbine's barrel with a ramrod, and snapping a percussion cap on the gun's nipple.

They were outnumbered seven men to God knew how many. The shots came fast from behind almost every tree. Leaves, branches, and pine needles flew off in every direction. Burke knew it was hopeless. "Mount up!" he yelled. The thick smell of sulfur from the black powder filled the air. White gunsmoke cut visibility to a few feet. Each man swung up into his saddle as best he could and lay low across his horse's neck. Some of the animals had also been hit.

Burke waved his arm around his head in a circle, then pointed downstream. He would take his men down to where the Scoobachita met the Zilpha. The squad took off following after the captain, chased by gunshots, until it disappeared around a bend in the creek. The entire affair lasted less than a minute.

Kirkland never made it. He had been hit several times; twice in the leg, once in his shoulder, and once in his arm and hand. His horse had galloped off the second Kirkland dropped the reins. He was seriously wounded, but still alive.

"Kirkland's down!" shouted Howard.

"I know," yelled Burke. "We'll have to get him later. Can't do nothin' now." The remainder of the squad turned west when it reached the juncture with the Zilpha, then made a wide circle south and east back towards Kosciusko. Kirkland's mount obediently followed the other horses.

The gunfire stopped as quickly as it began. The meadow was quiet once again, except for the groans from Private Kirkland. Slowly a group of men emerged from the woods. It was a large group, and each man in it carried a gun. There were squirrel guns, rifles, old flintlocks, muskets, and shotguns. They all had done their work. The men surrounded Kirkland who lay on his back bleeding badly. The guttural sounds he made came from deep within his belly. His mouth was open, and his eyes partially closed.

One of the men said, "Leave him." As the group of men melted back into the woods, a young man left the circle and disappeared into the trees. A short time later Albert Mitchell, along with the young man, drove his wagon into the clearing. Without saying a word the two men gently lifted the injured Kirkland into the bed of the wagon. The young man then ran off into the thicket.

Albert Mitchell was an old man, well into his sixties. He and his wife Sally lived in a small cabin buried in the forest near the Scoobachita. He hadn't been among the men who had fired on the cavalry squad, it wasn't his fight. But he knew what had to be done. He drove back to his cabin, and with the help of his wife took Kirkland inside. There the two of them ministered the man's wounds as best they could, applying poultices and cloth wraps wherever needed. Sally Mitchell used moss, clay, and herbs, as she had learned from her grandmother, to sooth the man's injuries and ease his pain. The bullet that hit Kirkland's hand went clean through it, and the one that hit his upper arm came close to the bone but didn't shatter it. His shoulder wound was more serious. It struck close to his neck and bled quickly. One of the bullets that hit his leg only clipped his thigh, but the other one lodged in the meaty part near his hip. Albert and Sally did what they could. It would have to do until they could seek help.

In the late afternoon when Burke and his battered squad arrived in Kosciusko he immediately went to the courthouse with his men. They were in pain, their clothes blood soaked. Logan himself was unhurt, save for his wounded pride for being caught in a surprise attack, but his uniform was shot through with several holes. Word had reached town ahead of the cavalrymen of some sort of dust up, and a crowd had gathered to find out what had happened. Massey was waiting outside.

"Report," Massey said in a sharp tone.

"Ambush, Captain. Up on the Scoobachita. Dozens of 'em, I'd say. Never saw it comin.' We took several hits as you can see," Burke said, as he watched his wounded being carried off. Massey said, "Take 'em to Doc Lewis or Galloway." The post hospital tent was far down past the cavalry camp. Lewis and Galloway had offices in town and could give his men the immediate attention they needed.

"Where's Kirkland?"

"Too badly wounded, sir. He got shot up pretty good. Had to leave him. We'll go back and get him, though." If he's alive, Burke thought to himself.

Massey was beside himself. Damnit, he fumed! Enough is enough! This will end. Someone will pay!

"See to your men, Captain." Massey lit another cigar and once again headed for Davis's Tavern.

# 5

# The Arrest

CAPTAIN MASSEY HAD NOT slept well the night before, even after his long visit to the tavern. Albert Mitchell, with his creaky one-horse wagon, had rolled into town around midnight. Massey, taking one look at the sorry sight of Kirkland lying in the back of the wagon, ordered Mitchell to take the man to Doctor Lewis. He figured the good doctor had patched up Burke's wounded well enough by then to be able to take on one more patient. Mitchell turned his wagon around and drove to the doctor's office. It was late, but the doctor was still awake. Lewis had worked on the injured troopers all night, removing bullets, cleaning wounds, stemming the flow of blood, and applying bandages. Mitchell and Lewis carried Kirkland inside. His job done, Mitchell headed back towards Liberty Chapel and home. But Massey wondered about him.

Massey tried to sleep. He had turned his headquarters office at the courthouse into his sleeping quarters, making himself as comfortable as he could. His bedroll was tucked into a corner of the room. Sleep didn't come easily, hardly at all. Massey spent most of the night staring at the flames burning in the small fireplace in his office. Come dawn, and after tossing the matter over in his head all night, he decided to take action. He would go up to the scene of the ambush and track down the bushwackers himself. But first he needed to file a report to his regimental commander, Colonel

William N. Brown, at the 20th Headquarters. Massey picked up his pen, dipped it in his ink jar, and began to write:

> *Colonel Wm. Brown, Comdr.*
> *Sept. 7, 1863*
> *Attala Co. Miss.*
> *20th Reg. Miss. Vol*
>
> *Sir*
>
> *Due to constant harassment of my command, and the firing upon my men, by bushwackers and army deserters in this county, I propose to lead a detachment myself for the purpose of clearing out the enemy once and for all.*
>
> *My cavalry has been shot at by these bandits and conscription evaders often. The latest ambush occurred yesterday, the result being the wounding of my men, some quite seriously.*
>
> *Please inform me of any further actions needed on my part.*
>
> *I am very respecfully*
> *Capt. C.K. Massey*
> *Comdr. Co. D 20th Reg. MVI*

Massey folded the paper, then walked from his office.

Captain Massey stood outside the courthouse the minute dawn broke over the town, and immediately called for Sergeant Turner. He was never far from the captain and followed Massey out the door.

"Sergeant, bring this dispatch to our cavalry courier. Have him take it to regimental headquarters at once. Then hitch the company wagon and bring it round here." Massey handed Turner his message. "Find Corporal Dolan. Tell him to get here right now." Almost as an afterthought he added, "And tell him to bring a length of rope. Maybe two."

"Yes sir." Massey wasn't finished. "Then find Captain Burke. Tell I want to see him, too."

"Anything else, sir?"

"That's all for now. Get movin'!"

Turner heard the urgency and tone in the captain's voice. He hurried towards the stables.

When Captain Burke got out of his bedroll he immediately saw Sergeant Turner sitting atop a wagon near the edge of the cavalry camp. Burke was still angry over yesterday's attack. He wanted revenge.

"What the hell is it now, Sergeant?" he called out.

"Cap'n wants you at the courthouse right now." Sergeant Turner had already given Massey's dispatch to the courier and relayed the captain's orders to Jimmy Dolan. "Hop in, Cap'n. I'll drive ya into town." Burke rammed his feet into his boots, pulled on his bullet riddled coat, snapped on his saber belt, and, without another word, climbed on board. Neither man spoke on the ride to the courthouse.

Corporal Dolan, rope in hand, stood by Captain Massey as Turner pulled the wagon to a stop in front of the courthouse. Massey began spitting out his orders.

"Captain Burke, I want you to get a patrol together. At least eight men, including anyone hit yesterday who can still ride. And get Wilson and Hart, too." Sick or not, Massey wanted them in the saddle. "Turner, Dolan, I want you in the wagon with me. Assemble back here in ten minutes."

Burke, on foot, ran back to the cavalry camp. "Saddle up, boys. Everyone!" he shouted. Looking at Wilson and Hart, standing outside their tent, he said, "And that means you two." Wilson gave a feeble cough for effect, but Burke said, "Not today. Massey wants everyone in line."

Captain Burke knew that other than Kirkland, all his men were serviceable. Cox's wound only grazed his thigh. Morgan and Douglass, though hit in their arms, could still wield a horse and hold a carbine. The bullet Douglass had received had been removed by Doctor Lewis. Their wounds were superficial; no bones were broken. That would've meant amputation. Howard and Ford were fine, and ready to go. If not for the lousy shots from the enemy, Burke thought, I wouldn't have a squad at all.

When the cavalry squad arrived at the courthouse Massey, Turner, and Dolan were already in the company wagon. Captain Massey checked his revolver, making sure all the chambers in the cylinder were loaded and capped off.

"Here's what's gonna happen," he said. "Captain Burke, I want you to take us back to where the skirmish took place. I want to find whoever was responsible for the ambush. You, and three of your men, will lead ahead of the wagon, and four will follow us."

Burke thought to himself, yes, we're finally going to clean out that nest of bushwackers. He and his men were still seething with anger over the attack. But he also wondered if they'd find anyone left in the area at all. Were they a day too late? "You heard the Captain, boys. Forward!"

It was still early in the morning. The air was crisp and cool, but the day's heat was rapidly approaching as the wagon, horses, and men rumbled out of town. Massey, and the ten men with him, had no idea what to expect.

The eight miles to the ambush site passed quietly. None of the men spoke as the small party travelled north from Kosciusko, following the path Burke and his men had taken the day before. Every man was watching the trees, woods, and forests around them with suspicious eyes. The only sounds heard were from a few jays fighting among the pines, and the creak of the wagon wheels over the rutted road. Their progress was slow. The wagon, pulled by two poorly nourished mules—fodder was hard to come by at this stage in the war—was making a slow go of it. The day heated up quickly.

Soon Howard, Ford, Cox, and Morgan—the four horsemen trailing Massey's wagon—began to grumble among themselves. Douglass, along with Hart, Wilson, and Burke, road ahead at the point. They were still fuming over the ambush from the day before. Their wounds still caused them pain, and the day's heat made their tempers flare.

Cox patted his holstered revolver as he looked down at his saber, which jangled by his side. "Kirkland's shot up real bad. We all been through the mill. Don't seem right we never got none a them."

"How d'ya know?" Ford asked. "Did'ja see any hits? Anyone go down?"

"Don't matter." Cox spit his tobacco juice over his horse's head. "Someone's gonna account for all of this, an' right now I don't give a shit who 'tis."

Howard wiped his dirty uniform sleeve across his brow. He missed his hat and wanted the damn thing back. "I'm with ya there," he said. Howard was armed with only his carbine. He didn't carry a side arm, nor a saber. He didn't care. He could reload, cap, and fire his weapon faster than anyone else in his squad. "Someone's gonna pay sure as I'm ridin' this nag."

"What say we fire an' ask questions later?" said Morgan. "They got what's comin' to 'em."

"Massey an' Burke would crap a mountain if we did," Ford said after taking a swig from his canteen.

"I don't give a rat's arse," Cox replied in an angry whisper. He looked at Captain Massey up ahead of them in the wagon. It was churning up clouds of dust in the soldiers' faces. "What's he gonna do? He don't like what happened any more'n we do. An' Burke don't neither. I say if we get the chance an' we come across any of them muggins we let loose. We say they were in on the attack. Who's to say it weren't so?"

The four men rode in silence for a while, each lost in his own thoughts. At last Ford said, "I'm in."

Howard, Ford, Cox, Morgan, Kirkland, and Douglass all hailed from Carroll County, just northwest of Attala. They grew up in and around the town of Vaiden, raised hell when they could, and paid for it with jail time. None of the men came from families of slave owners—they were all dirt poor—but they also saw nothing wrong with owning a black man. And more to the point, the six men were irritated to no end by seeing free blacks roaming the county.

When secession, then war, came to the South it was Cox who stirred their passions up to a frenzy and convinced the other five to enlist. It didn't take much convincing. They were all lost in war fever. They joined the 20th as infantry privates but were quickly moved to a mounted unit due to their familiarity with horses. They were all farm boys, and the fact that several of the men brought their own mounts with them sealed their fate as cavalry.

This brought them into Logan Burke's orbit when they were assigned to his cavalry unit. They detested the man and his holier-than-thou attitude. The six men disliked Conrad Massey only a bit less. They had wanted to serve with other men from Carroll County, many of them their friends and neighbors. Being sent to Burke's unit, and under Massey's command, didn't sit well with them at all. All six men weren't happy with being stuck in this backwater of the war. They wanted to be in Virginia with Lee's Army of Northern Virginia, or, at the very least with Braxton Bragg in Georgia. The godawful patrol they were on now only made things worse.

"Halt!" Captain Burke raised his hand in the air as a signal to the others. They had stopped at the Scoobachita. Burke looked around him at the creek, the meadow, and the surrounding trees. "This is it, Captain." He was amazed. All was quiet. You'd never know that anything had ever happened here the day before, he thought. No spilled blood, no empty cartridge papers lying about. Even Howard's hat, shot off his head yesterday, was missing. They probably took it as a prize, he said to himself.

"You sure?" Massey asked.

"Positive, Captain. Can't explain why this place is lookin' so clean, though."

"Don't matter. Post your men, Captain. Everyone at the ready. Keep a sharp eye. Take three men, Burke, and head up yonder." A small trail, barely larger than the width of a wagon, led off into the pines from the creek.

"Howard, Ford, Wilson, follow me," Burke ordered. "The rest of you dismount and form a circle around the wagon."

As Burke and his men disappeared down the trail, their horses leaving clouds of dust behind them, Massey turned to Sergeant Turner and Corporal Dolan. "Let's get down off a here. We're easy targets." Turner and Dolan were only too happy to oblige. They climbed down, but stayed close to the wagon, ready to duck under it at the first sign of trouble. Turner and Dolan's rifles were capped and the hammers in the half cock position. They were each armed with a British made Enfield .57 caliber rifle-musket. All of Massey's infantry in Company D were armed with the .57. Massey crouched by one of the wagon's forward wheels.

The day heated up. There was no shade to be had in the clearing, and Massey considered allowing the men to find some relief among the trees. It would be risky. Worse than remaining here in the open? Maybe. But it was so still. There was no movement in the trees, at least as best he could tell. He finally came to a decision. "Water your horses, men, and yourselves. Take turns grabbing some shade. Go in twos. Stay alert." The men did as they were told but found the shade almost as suffocating as the sun.

About forty minutes had passed when the sound of horses was heard coming down the little trail. Everyone was on edge. Hands gripped tighter around weapons. Perspiration dripped from each man's brow.

It was Burke, Howard, Ford, and Wilson. With them was an old man walking in front of the horses. It was Albert Mitchell. He ain't the old man from Possumneck, Burke said to himself, but he'll do.

Captain Burke and his three-man escort had followed the path deep into the woods until it finally ended at a little log cabin surrounded by a cluster of tall pine trees. A wisp of smoke could be seen trailing up from a stone chimney.

Burke dismounted and stepped onto the wood porch, then pounded on the door. "Open up!" he yelled. Immediately the door was opened by a short plump woman. Her gray hair was pulled back into a tight bun at the back of her head. She wore a plain unadorned gray dress. The worn threads at the seams showed its age. Her smudged white apron was tied across her neck and around her waist. This was Sally Mitchell. Before she could offer a greeting, Burke said loudly, "We need to see your husband."

Albert Mitchell came to the door. "Yes sir. What can I do fer ya? Me an' the missus were jus settin' down to a meal."

Burke, his tone a little more mellow upon seeing the old man's wife, said, "You need to come with us."

"Fer what?" Mitchell was confused and completely taken by surprise.

"You'll find out in good order."

Sally turned to her husband. "Albert, what's this all about?"

"Don't know, Sal. But if I don't go with these here soldiers it could be the worse fer us. Don'tcha worry now. I'm sure I'll be back shortly." Sally put a hand over her mouth. Her eyes welled up with tears. With a kiss on her forehead, Mitchell turned to Burke and said, "Let's go."

"Keep in front of my squad," Burke said, "an' don't try somethin' you'll regret." Mitchell thought to himself, I'm almost seventy. What could I possibly do?

"Looky what we got here, Captain," Burke said smiling as his squad came to a halt. Massey had been crouching beside one of the wagon wheels along with Tuner and Dolan. He stood. "Mitchell!" he said, almost as a question.

"That's me. Seems like I jus saw ya last night. What's this all about? Your gang, here, grabbed me right there in my own home, right in front of my wife."

Massey had to think fast. Could this man have been a part of the ambush? This old man? But he brought the wounded Kirkland into town. Still, he might have been involved. Massey would take no chances.

"Mitchell, you're under arrest."

"And fer what, Captain?"

"For the attack on my men yesterday."

Mitchell, stooped at the shoulders, rubbed his long white beard and wiped his forehead with a ragged handkerchief. His torn slouch hat barely offered cover from the sun, and his unruly snow-white hair poked through its many holes. "Yer makin' a mistake there, Captain."

Massey knew he probably had but continued anyway. "That'll be determined after we take you back to town. Bind his hands, Corporal." Corporal Dolan, still holding the rope, pulled Mitchell's arms behind his back and tied his hands.

"Lift him into the back of the wagon," Massey said. "Captain Burke, have your men mount up." Turner and Dolan helped the old man aboard, then took their place next to Massey on the wagon's bench seat.

"Back to town, Captain?" Burke asked.

Massey knew that staying where they were was a waste of time. They weren't going to find anyone else here. Those people had drifted away like leaves in the wind. "No, there's one more stop I want to make."

Nathan Sweatt had just finished his work in the fields. He and his children—Mary, James, Amanda, and John—were done for the day. The heat was brutal. They would wash up and go inside for their mid-day meal. His two oldest daughters, Easter and Margaret, were already helping their mother with dinner. Little Cicero, the youngest child, remained inside with them. Nathan was in his shirtsleeves and wore a wide brim straw hat to keep the sun from his head. He and his children had tilled their fields by hand, getting them ready for the next planting.

As he stopped at the well beside the house Nathan wiped his brow with his handkerchief, took a deep breath, and let out a long sigh. When he looked around him—at the fields, at his wood frame house, at his children—he thought in wonder, and told himself, that this, with God's help, I did on my own. He was lucky, he knew. The war hadn't touched him the way it had some of his neighbors. Had the military been told to spare his farm? Perhaps the men roaming the countryside knew him well enough that he and his family would be left alone. Whatever the reason, the Reverend knew he was fortunate.

Nathan and his children walked into the house. A huge magnolia tree and some dogwoods gave shade to their home. They walked past the parlor and into the kitchen.

Margaret Sweatt kept a well run kitchen. These were hard times, but with God's help and her family's hard work they had managed to keep her pantry, if not fully stocked, at least full enough for their needs. A small cast-iron woodburning stove stood along one wall, and pantry shelves along another. All her iron pots and pans—brought with the family from Georgia—hung neatly from pegs above the stove. The warm smell of cooked food filled the air.

Margaret and her daughters had set the long table with a bounty of food. They had laid out a platter of roasted chicken, fresh baked bread, corn, and a bowl of green beans. The Reverend and his family gathered round the table, sat down, then held each other's hand in an unbroken circle. They bowed their heads.

"Dear Lord," Nathan began, "we ask you to bless this food which we are about to eat, which we planted with our own hands, and harvested with our own toil and hard work. We ask that you protect those of us here at your table with your loving hands and protect those who cannot be here today." He paused, thinking of William and Nathan, then continued. "We also pray for our son, Lewis, who you took to your bosom at such a young age. We know he rests with you in your kingdom forever." Lewis had died in 1858 from pneumonia at the age of six. "We ask this through Christ, our Lord, Amen." His family repeated, "Amen."

As his family passed the bowls and plates of food around the table Nathan looked at his wife, Margaret, and smiled. Their second oldest daughter, also named Margaret, though they called her by her middle name Jennie—Jen, for short—sat next to her mother. They are so much alike, thought Nathan. Jen had the small spare figure of her mother, the olive skin, the black hair, and the large dark eyes. He looked around the table at each of his children. Yes, he told himself, God has truly blessed us.

Cicero suddenly turned to his father and asked, "Pa, what happened yesterday? Why was there a fight out by the creek? Did you see anything? Was anybody hurt?"

"Son, I was here all day long. I don't know what happened or why it happened. And yes, someone got hurt." He knew this from the night before. "There are bad men hiding in the woods. They don't like the soldiers and the soldiers don't like them. And sometimes they fight each other." Nathan looked around the table.

"That's why I keep reminding you children to stay close to home. Don't go off traipsing in the woods. We don't want trouble. We stick to ourselves."

Margaret quickly changed the subject. "Are you finished writing Sunday's sermon, Nathan?"

"Will put the final touches on it tonight, Marg." The Reverend would begin writing the next week's sermon almost as soon as he delivered the last one.

The family was just about finished with their meal when they heard a pounding on the front door. Lord, who could that be, Nathan wondered. He rose from the table and opened the door.

There, on his step, stood Captain Massey. On one side of him stood a sergeant. On the other, a smaller man holding a coil of rope. The Reverend recognized those two from his Sunday service. Beyond them, in the yard, was a wagon surrounded by eight mounted men. He saw Albert Mitchell sitting in the back of the wagon.

"Can I help you, Captain?" asked Nathan.

"I 'spose you heard 'bout the skirmish out by the Scoobachita?"

"Yes, very unfortunate. What does that have to do with me?"

"I'll get right to it, Reverend. Where were you yesterday 'bout mid-morning," Massey said in a strong voice.

"Right here, working the fields with my family." Nathan could see where this was going. "I can be vouched for."

"Of course you can," said Massey, a tinge of sarcasm in his voice. "What else would your family say?"

"What do you want?" Nathan's wife had come up beside him and put her arm through his.

"I'm putting you under arrest," Massey said with all the authority he could muster. In the back of his mind he knew this was thin stuff. "For inciting guerrilla activity and hiding your sons from military service."

"This is ridiculous," Nathan said, "and you know it! I've told you already I don't know where my sons are."

"Sorry Reverend, you're comin' with us." Without another word Sergeant Turner grabbed Nathan and pulled him out of the house. Corporal Dolan took his rope and quickly tied the Reverend's hands behind his back.

"No!" screamed Margaret in panic. The other children had now crowded the doorway. "No!" screamed Margaret again.

Nathan, held by his arms between the two soldiers, turned to his wife and family. "Marg, it will be all right. This will be straightened out. I will be home soon. I trust in the Lord. You need to, also. All of you," he said in a calm voice.

The Reverend was put in the wagon next to Mitchell. Nathan's family, in tears, watched as the wagon pulled out of the yard and into the road.

Captain Burke rode up alongside the wagon and looked down at Albert Mitchell and Nathan Sweatt. "Gonna miss that little mulatto wife of yours, Preacher?" Burke sneered with a laugh. "Right fine little lady ya got there."

Nathan ignored him, and recited Psalm 23 softly. The man's a fool, Nathan said to himself. Margaret was of Cherokee blood.

# 6

# The Guardhouse

THE RIDE BACK INTO town was long and slow. The two mules pulling the wagon were just about played out. The heat had affected both animals and men alike. Nathan Sweatt and Albert Mitchell were extremely stressed on the return trip. With hands tied and sitting in the bed of the wagon every jarring bounce over the uneven road proved an ordeal in agony. The two men were tossed around like loose marbles. They each tried to brace themselves by jamming their feet against the opposite side of the wagon to stabilize their bodies. This only worked until the wagon made another heaving lurch to one side or the other, then they would roll back and forth once again.

After repeating the Psalm to himself, Nathan began to think. He was in a dangerous situation considering all that was at stake. His shirt was wet with perspiration, it trickled off his head and down his face and back. He had tried to reassure Margaret and his family that everything would work out. That when the facts had been examined by Captain Massey, and with his explanation of where he was and what he had been doing at the time of the ambush, everything would fall into place and he would be released. But would that be the outcome? It was his word against the captain's and when he saw that the only two people Massey could produce from his bushwacker hunt were Albert and himself it became clear that the captain wanted something to show for it.

Military justice could be swift and unfair. Civilians in an occupied town, North or South, had little to no authority. Nathan and Albert were at the mercy of Captain Massey and the 20th Mississippi. Civilian laws were pretty much tossed aside. It wouldn't be a matter of Captain Massey and the army having to prove them guilty. No, Nathan and Albert would need to prove they were innocent. And what would happen to Margaret and the children? They would be left to tend to the farm themselves. Would they face retribution? What kind of man was the captain? Would he come down hard on Margaret, trying to force an explanation as to the whereabouts of William and Nate? She doesn't know where our two sons are any more than I do. Would Massey wipe out his farm and crops in an effort to put pressure on his family to get what he wanted? Nathan trusted in the Lord, but not in Captain Massey, and he had a terrible dread in the pit of his stomach.

Albert Mitchell suffered the wagon ride in silence. He had very little to lose. He and his wife were poor dirt farmers, and losing what they had was almost the same as having nothing at all. He was worried sick, though, about Sally.

It was late in the afternoon when Captain Massey's small military caravan pulled into Kosciusko and stopped at the courthouse. The sun was setting, and the earth was slowly cooling, but it was still uncomfortably warm. The men in Captain Burke's cavalry escort who had been wounded in the ambush the day before were dismissed to either go back to their camp or seek further treatment at the doctor's office if they needed it. Most of them were hurting and weary to the bone. Those not wounded were ordered to stay at the courthouse until the two prisoners were secured inside. The two men were helped down from the wagon, their hands still tied.

The Reverend Sweatt finally spoke. "Captain, I'd be much obliged if you could unbind these ropes. I will not flee, and they're mighty tight about me."

"They're givin' me a pinch, too," said Mitchell.

Massey turned to Jimmy Dolan. "Corporal, untie these two and escort 'em into the guardhouse."

Nathan Sweatt faced the captain. "This town has its own jail, sir." He would rather be in the custody of Sheriff Noah than under the army's thumb.

"This is a military matter. The town jail is for drunks, vagrants, and thieves. You are both under my authority."

The Reverend and Mitchell both rubbed their wrists as they walked through the courthouse doors. Massey then faced the sergeant. "Turner, I want a twenty-four hour watch on the prisoners. All doors leadin' to the courtroom are to be secured and guarded at all times. No one goes in or out without my permission. Understood?"

"Yes sir." Turner left to tell Dolan to stay with the two men until he could round up a guard detail and schedule the men into four hour shifts.

As the rest of the cavalry squad disbursed to return to their camp, Massey walked inside the courthouse to talk with his prisoners. Mitchell and the Reverend were sitting side by side in the courtroom gallery. The gallery was separated from the judge's bench by a wooden railing. Two tables, each with a couple of chairs beside them, stood in front of the bench. The jury box was to the left of the judge's bench.

"You will both remain here, under guard, 'til my investigation is complete. You will be provided food and bedding," Massey said matter-of-factly.

"Will we be allowed visitors?" Nathan asked in his low, quiet voice.

"That remains to be seen." With that, Massey left and returned to his office next to the courtroom.

A squad of soldiers from Company D had already appeared and stationed themselves outside the courtroom's four doors, locking them, and posting a man at each one. All the guards stood with their rifles by their sides.

Shortly a private—an orderly—arrived carrying two plates of food; salt pork and hardtack, pretty hard fare to be sure. Army rations. Neither man touched it. Massey could have done better.

His commissary officer, Captain Parr—also subject to Massey's orders—sat on a large store of food in town. It would only be issued at the discretion of Captain C.K. Massey. The orderly soon returned holding an armful of blankets and straw. Without saying a word he dropped them on the floor and left.

"I don't mind tellin' ya, Reverend, I'm scared," said Mitchell. "I don't know who them men were that done the shootin'. All I know is a young fella comes runnin' up to my cabin an' tells me to bring my wagon quick. Guess he's a bushwacker with a conscience." Mitchell chuckled a little at this. "The missus an' me patched that soldier up a bit, then I brought him to your place last night. It was you, Reverend, told me to take him into town." Mitchell was twisting his battered hat in his hands. "Tried to do right by the man. Now look what it got me."

"You did the right thing, Albert," Nathan said with a little smile on his face. "God knows you did, and so do I."

"Reverend, you and your family been right nice to me an' Sally. Ya'll been good neighbors. Ya'll shared your bounty with me an' Sal when we got stretched pretty thin. We'll always be in your debt." Mitchell teared up. "You don't look at me as that crazy hermit livin' in the forest, like some townfolk do."

Nathan looked at Mitchell square in the eyes. "Albert, you owe us nothing. I know you and Sally would do the same for us if you could. I see the both of you at every Sunday service. You're a God-fearing man who lives by His rule. A good man, Albert."

The Reverend put his hand on Mitchell's shoulder and began softly, "The Lord is my light and my salvation; whom shall I fear? When evil men come to destroy me, they will stumble and fall! Yes, though a mighty army marches against me, my heart shall know no fear! I am confident that God will save me."

Massey, ensconced in his office, figured he had another sleepless night ahead of him. His mind kept turning over what he knew. Holding Albert Mitchell any longer was useless. The man was ancient, posed no threat to the army, lived a solitary life buried in the woods, and, if nothing else, came to the rescue of one of Burke's men. Any charges against him wouldn't hold in the wash. He'd be released in the morning. The Reverend was a different matter, though.

The whole damn county was Union leaning, as Massey figured it. Everyone seemed to love the preacher. But he had a good case against the Reverend Sweatt, Massey thought. Hiding his two draft age sons—somewhere—was a good start. And that letter to the newspaper . . .

I'll get it out of him, the captain said to himself. And aiding or abetting guerrilla activity should stick. He was in the area, no matter what his family might say, and at any rate he had to know what happened and who was there. "Yes," Massey said out loud, "he'll stay in the guardhouse for a while."

The next day the visitors came in a steady stream. Margaret arrived early the next morning. Her son James helped her to hitch the family wagon, and, with her family in tow, drove into town. When they stopped at the courthouse Margaret headed straight to Massey's office, walking right past the guards at the front door.

"I want to see my husband," she said without so much as a hello. It was more a demand than a request.

"Well, I think we can work that out," Massey replied. "You only, though."

"What about his children?"

"Sorry, ma'am. You only."

Margaret told her children to come into Massey's office. They climbed down from the wagon, and soon his office was crammed with the Reverend's family. And Massey didn't like it. "At least they can see their father from the doorway," she said, looking at the captain. "Will that do?"

Massey grudgingly agreed and ordered the guard to open the courtroom door. As he did so Massey added, "And bring Mitchell out here."

As the children gathered at the doorway, Margaret walked in passing Mitchell on his way out. Without saying a word she gently touched his arm and looked him in the eye. He nodded his head in an unspoken reply.

Margaret carried a small cloth bundle with her. The guard had examined it and said to Massey, "It's good."

Nathan Sweatt put his arms around his wife and said, "Are you alright? Are the children?"

"Yes, we're fine, at least as best we can be. Do you know how long they're keeping you?"

"I don't know, Marg. I don't see how they can charge me with anything. You know it, I know it, and he knows it," Nathan said as he nodded his head at Massey's office. "They're looking for someone to paint this on. It's revenge pure and simple."

"I brought you something to eat," Margaret said, as she unwrapped her bundle of cold chicken, bread, and some corn. "And this." She pulled out of her apron pocket Nathan's Bible and handed it to him.

"Thank you," he said, looking at the book, then at his wife. "You, my family, and this will get me through."

When Margaret and her children left the courthouse, they saw Albert Mitchell standing next to their wagon.

"Would it be too much to ask for a ride back to my cabin?" Mitchell asked in a humble voice.

"Albert, I'd be more than happy to do so."

Not long after Margaret drove away, George Harlow, the *Chronicle* editor, arrived at the courthouse. "I'd like to see the Reverend," he told Massey.

"You, too?" Massey said with some sarcasm.

"That's correct, there, Captain. Go ahead an' search me."

Harlow sat down next to Nathan after the guard had unlocked the door to let him in. "How ya doin', Nate?" Harlow asked.

"Fair to middlin', George. I guess it's as best as I could hope for all things considered."

"Can I get ya anything? Is there somethin' ya need?"

"No, but I do thank you, George, for your concern. I'm just hoping my stay here is a short one."

"Well, I gotta tell ya, Nate, most the whole town is behind ya. Everyone knows this stinks fer sure. Word of that little skirmish up at the creek spread 'round here right quick. And yer arrest? Even quicker."

Nathan had to chuckle a little to himself. He'd known George Harlow for years and was always amazed that someone so educated could publish a newspaper, be its editor, yet could speak as though he came right out of the backwoods of the Appalachians.

"That's comforting to know, George, though it really doesn't affect my current situation, now does it?"

"No, it surely don't. But I thought it'd be good for ya to know."

"Thank you, George. It is."

When Jonah Davis showed up at the courthouse Captain Massey thought to himself, Christ, another one? Will this day never end?

Davis was allowed in after being searched by the guard. He walked up to Nathan. "I'm sure sorry you're here, Reverend."

Nathan knew Jonah Davis, but not well. Davis would, on occasion, attend a Sunday service or two, but mostly stayed away. Nathan thought that Davis, perhaps embarrassed by the type of establishment he ran, had a guilty conscience.

"Jonah, thank you for that. I hope you're doing well."

"I brought a little somethin', Mr. Sweatt." With that Davis pulled from his boot a small flask and a somewhat crumpled cigar. The guard's haphazard search failed to find the two items. "I know it ain't much, but I'm figurin' it could help pass the time."

"I do appreciate the gesture, Jonah, but I can't accept them." Nathan let a small smile pass his face. I'm a Methodist minister, he said to himself. Davis knows that. "Jonah, it just won't do. Once the captain or the guards find out we'll both be in for it. I do thank you anyway."

"I figured as such," said Davis sheepishly. It was the best he could do. "You take care, now, Reverend."

"I will."

Nathan Sweatt spent the rest of the day eating what Margaret had brought him and reading his Bible. He asked nothing of Captain Massey.

Other than talking to his friends and visitors, Nathan kept to himself. Captain Massey rarely came to check on the Reverend, preferring instead to ask the courthouse guards if all was well with his prisoner. Nathan didn't mind the solitude. Being left to his thoughts and prayers was preferable to anything he could gain or accomplish with the captain.

The same orderly who had brought straw, blankets, and food to Albert Mitchell and himself on the day of their arrest was the one constant face he would see of the military over many days. Their only exchange when his food was brought in amounted to a "thank you" from Nathan and a nod of the head from the soldier. But Nathan became curious.

The guard, a fresh-faced youngster who looked nineteen, if that, became a little more talkative with each visit. He soon was asking the Reverend if there was anything he needed. Was there something more he could bring him? Nathan would answer "no" and thank the orderly. But one day Nathan asked the boy his name.

The orderly had just delivered another plate of the scanty food, along with a fresh cup of water, and had begun to leave. He picked up the used plate and cup and turned to look at the Reverend. His eyes were wide as he looked at Nathan, then back towards Massey's office.

"It's all right, son. I don't believe the captain is home right now. What's your name?" Nathan asked again.

"Thomas," the boy said almost sheepishly.

"Thomas. That's my son's name. Well actually, it's his middle name. My wife and I chose the name because Thomas was one of the Apostles of Jesus. He became known as 'Doubting Thomas' because he questioned the resurrection of Jesus. He became a believer when he saw the wounds on the hands and feet of the resurrected Jesus after his crucifixion. Did you know that?"

The orderly uttered a quiet "No." Then he added, "Never had much religion learnin', I guess."

"No matter," Nathan said. "Where are you from, Thomas?"

Relaxing a little, the young soldier answered, "Bolivar County, sir. That's where I enlisted."

"Bolivar? Never been over that way. You're near the river. Does your family farm?"

"Yes sir. We got a farm there by the Mississippi. Just me an' my pa and two brothers." Thomas looked down at his feet then back at Nathan. "Ma's been dead 'bout five years now. Just the four of us." The boy seemed to want to talk. "I guess now it's just Pa and Elliot. He's my youngest brother. Me an' Frank, we enlisted. Don't know where he is now. Probably with the rest of the Twentieh somewhere."

Nathan looked at Thomas for a while. "How old are you, son?"

"Seventeen. I'm the middle one. Frank's twenty."

"Why did you join up?" Nathan said this with genuine curiosity.

Thomas became a bit excited when he answered. "To fight them Yankees. They be takin' our land."

The Reverend Sweatt thought for a second. "Your family farm, just your brothers and you working it with your father? You don't own any slaves?"

Thomas sounded a little indignant, as though the pastor had insulted him. "Course not! We're pretty hard scrabble to tell the truth. Barely get by as is." A confused look came upon his face. "Don't know why them abolitionists want to fight us." Thomas became less agitated when he added, "Was right excited when first I joined. Don't seem so much now."

"Do you miss home?" Nathan said in a soft voice. The boy in front of him looked forlorn and lost. Standing there in a shabby and ill-fitting uniform, he looked much younger than his seventeen years.

"I miss it terrible. This soldierin' is a might tryin'. I could give it up in a blink."

"I miss my son Thomas and his brother Nathan very much. I haven't seen them in years." Nathan looked at the orderly with sad eyes.

"Are they in the army?" asked Thomas.

"No. They're gone because they don't want to fight. They don't believe in this war. They don't believe in killing." Nathan paused, then added, "They don't believe in slavery. That's why they lit out. And I don't know where they are, Thomas."

Thomas thought for a second. "Slavery? I don't give a whit 'bout that neither." He said this in a quiet voice as he looked towards Massey's office again. "We been workin' our farm ourselves. Don't need no slavery to do it."

Nathan stared directly at the boy. "Thomas, that's what this war is all about. You've already told me your family doesn't own any slaves. This is from the Bible, son. 'Live as people who are free, not using your freedom as a cover-up for evil, but living as servants of God.'" The orderly didn't reply, so Nathan continued. "Listen, Thomas, 'For freedom Christ has set us free; stand firm therefore, and do not submit again to a yoke of slavery.'" Again, the boy stood silent.

Thomas set the empty tin plate and cup on the floor. "Are you sayin' this whole shebang's 'bout freein' the black man? That the blue boys ain't 'bout takin' our farm?"

"Well, that's at least the kernel in this entire thing. Keeping the country whole isn't a bad thing, don't you think?"

Thomas took off his hat and scratched his head. "I never owned nobody, an' never killed nobody in my life. Seems like a waste." He looked at the Reverend. "These here are thoughts I never chewed on before. I got some tolerable thinkin' to do."

Nathan let a smile cross his face. "Having some doubts, there, Thomas?"

The young soldier gave Nathan a confused look. "I reckon you might be right, Reverend. I'm gonna set myself on this for a might. I best be goin'. You won't be tellin' Captain Massey 'bout none a this, will you?"

Nathan walked over to Thomas and put his hand on the boy's shoulder. "Not a word, son."

# 7

# The Other Prisoner

LEWIS BRYANT WAS NOT an army deserter for the simple reason that he had never been in the army. Nor was he a bushwacker, bandit, or renegade—at least in his mind. He was, he knew, a draft evader. He had been dodging and evading conscription by Confederate authorities, the Home Guard, and the county sheriff ever since he had received a draft notice in April of 1862. He had lived alone on his little farm northwest of Kosciusko from the time his parents died until he was informed he had to report to the army. From then on he had been on the run.

Bryant owned no slaves, so he couldn't use that as a reason to avoid conscription. A person had to own twenty slaves to be exempt from military service. Bryant was also poor, so he knew he couldn't pay to hire a substitute to take his place in the army. His last remaining option was to disappear into the woods, and for more than a year that's exactly what he had been doing. He would sleep under the stars, sometimes in the rain, and live off the land.

Lewis Bryant didn't want to face any Yankees. This was a rich man's war and a poor man's fight, and he had no desire to stick his neck out so that some fat plantation owner could keep his slaves. No, he'd take his chances on his own. With only the clothes on his back and a sack of whatever food he could carry, he lit out into the forests of Attala County. He also made sure to bring his squirrel gun.

Bryant was a tall, skinny boy of nineteen. His dark eyes matched his unruly black hair. His coarse woolen pants were held up with threadbare braces, and his faded blue checkered shirt was covered with a brown patched coat. He made sure his black slouch hat always sat at a jaunty angle on his head. Lewis Bryant was wise to the game, cocky, shrewd, and quick on his feet. He had no trouble stretching the truth whenever it needed to be stretched.

Hiding, dodging, and moving about the woods on his own, trying to stay one step ahead of the authorities, was time-consuming and tiresome. He'd hunt game—usually rabbits, squirrels, and an occasional turkey—and fish for his meals. Sometimes he would barter with a runaway slave or another vagrant like himself. He'd trade whatever he caught for some tobacco or coffee, but the constant moving about and hiding by day or night on his own was taking its toll. Lewis Bryant needed a family. When he stumbled across a group of men camped in the woods south of New Hope Church he thought he'd found one.

His approach was heard before he even appeared. Every man around the campfire grabbed his gun and stood. When Lewis Bryant emerged from the brush he was looking down the barrels of ten rifles.

"That's fer enuf. Who ya be?" A tall, broad-shouldered and heavily bearded man took aim at Bryant.

"Hold there!" Lewis yelled. He kept his rifle down by his side. He didn't want to start a fight he knew he'd lose. "I mean no trouble to ya'll. Just passin' through. Heard some talk an' smelled some smoke. Name's Wade. Calvin Wade. Ya can call me Cal, if'n it's all the same to you." Bryant wasn't about to use his real name. He didn't know who these men were. "Looks like ya got yerself some chicory, there. I'd be much obliged if I could taste a cup or two."

"Are ya army?" the bearded man asked.

"No, not likely." Bryant said this as friendly as he could. He could tell these men weren't army and wanted no part of the military.

Without saying a word, the tall man looked at the others, then nodded his head towards the fire. This kid didn't appear to be a threat. If he was he'd be dead before he hit the ground. The men sat back down, but kept their guns close by. Lewis Bryant had found his family. This is where he belonged.

The tall bearded man looked at the others around the campfire. "Gotta do better on outpost. This here fella got the jump on us. Never should'a come this close."

It soon became apparent to Bryant who these men were. These were the bushwackers—the bandits, the deserters—he had heard rumors of during his months on the run. He was surprised he hadn't come across them in all the time since he'd left his farm. But the county was large, and the forests, hollows, brush, and thickets were numerous. It was obvious to Lewis Bryant that these men had banded together for their own protection.

In time the other men in the group of runaways came to accept Bryant. They addressed each other by their first names only. Lewis understood this was for their own safety, and he figured they weren't using their real names anyway. He wasn't either, so he'd stick with Calvin. None of the men wore any semblance of a Confederate uniform. Those had been discarded long ago. Being caught in one was a sure death sentence by hanging or firing squad. Being caught in civilian clothes meant, at best, a person would be tagged as evading the draft.

The men never remained in one place for long. They would move their camp regularly, staying deep in the woods, and never return to the same campsite twice. This kept the cavalry patrols guessing. The horse soldiers would find remnants of a fire pit long after the men had left.

Lewis Bryant learned that some of these men were army deserters. Some were dodging conscription, some were army stragglers hesitant to return to their regiments, and a few were simply guerrillas preying on whatever and whomever they could. Bryant would keep behind his façade. He had no desire to rob or kill anyone—that was the whole point of dodging the draft. When the group went out on one of its sorties, Lewis would remain behind, sometimes with others, and guard the camp. He'd hunt with the men for their food, and act as a lookout if needed.

Bryant also learned the stories of a few of the men, whenever they chose to talk. He had no idea if any of what he heard was true. Probably very little. The big bearded man's name was Jock, or so he called himself. He said he had left Joe Johnston and the army when the general had evacuated Jackson back in May. He was content to ride out the war where he was. He wasn't about to volunteer any more information to Bryant than he already had.

"What's yer story, Wade?" Jock wanted to probe, and this shavetail seemed to want to talk.

"Well, I was at Vicksburg with Pemberton and his army. Was in the Thirty-seventh Mississippi, Holland's Regiment in Herbert's Brigade. All part of General Forney's Division. I gotta tell ya, 'tween Grant and Sherman they had us boxed in purdy darn good." Bryant had no idea if the 37th was even at Vicksburg. Everything he was telling Jock he had gotten from months-old newspapers he had picked up in his travels. It was all a cover.

"How'd ya find yerself here?"

The lies began to snowball. "I could see what was 'bout to happen. We was down to eatin' rats there near the end. Me an' some of my messmates figured we'd be livin' in a Yankee prison camp soon as the noose cinched up an' we surrendered. Weren't havin' none of that. So we decided to get out any way we could. We dug ourselves out of our trenches one night on the river side of town. We split up. Don't know where them others went, but I took off with nothin' but my squirrel gun here an' the clothes on my back."

Jock didn't say a thing. He looked at Lewis and simply nodded his head. Lewis added to his story. "I travelled by night, see, an' hugged the Mississippi shore, hunkerin' down whenever I saw or heard a thing. Them Yanks couldn't see me a'tall. Then I just made a wide circle 'round any Federals I seed an' come on back to Attala." Lewis was proud of his tale of escape. It was one of the best stories he'd ever told. Jock didn't believe a word of it, but let it pass. All he said was, "Hellava story, Cal."

One of the men sitting around the fire, a short mean looking man with few teeth and a huge knife tucked under his belt, spit into the flames and said, "Yeah, hellava tale, there, kid. Surprised ya didn't take on the whole damn Yankee army by yerself." Bryant didn't say a word, but only stared down at the fire.

It was Lewis Bryant's turn to stand guard outside the camp on October 2. He picked up his rifle and quietly and slowly made his way through the thick forest of trees. The weather was damp, and he was cold. He wished he could have remained by the fire in camp, but he knew this was his duty, especially if he wanted to keep on good terms with the others.

He had carefully walked several miles from the campsite making sure to tread softly over the pine needles and branches scattered across the forest floor. The smell of wet pine filled the air. He knew he was close by New Hope Church but didn't dare expose himself. Bryant, however, was tired of being crowded by the woods. The trees, so close together, were like walls surrounding and suffocating him. He wanted a breath of clear air, to feel a breeze against his face, even if just for a moment. With that he stepped out of the forest and onto a muddy road.

Captain Logan Burke decided it was time for another patrol around the county. It was October 2, and he figured a sweep southwest of Kosciusko would be in order. Maybe towards Newport. He could then head east, cross the Yockanookany, ride north through New Hope Church, and finally west over the Yock again and the Natchez Trace, then back to town. Even though the ambush of his men happened almost a month ago, he didn't want to take any of his troopers who had been caught in the crossfire. Let 'em heal up some more. They had done their job. He would build this squad from men he had assigned to "light duty," as he called it—small patrols in and around town.

"Porter, Kendall, Monroe, Jackson! Get yer gear, get yer mounts, and be back here in five minutes." Burke was standing outside his tent holding up his uniform coat and examining the bullet holes in it. Damn that was close, he said to himself. There were rips in the sleeves, shoulder, and collar. He knew he had been lucky. "Kendall, Porter, bring the dogs this time."

Private Josh Kendall was not too happy about Burke's patrol assignment. He had been more than happy, though, with his duty around town. He could go where he pleased, talk to the young ladies he passed, and even sneak a drink at the tavern now and then. It was off-limits to enlisted men, of course. Galloping about the county and getting shot at was not something he looked forward to. Kendall was a short thin boy of eighteen. He had enlisted right after he turned of age and was mustered into the cavalry due to his skill on horseback. It helped being raised on a farm. He didn't give a skosh about abolition, Unionism, or slavery—his family did own a considerable number of slaves—no, all he cared about was the glory and the excitement of the cavalry. Even with the Union occupation of almost all of Mississippi, Kendall's family still had enough money to equip him above and beyond the average Confederate soldier. This was fine with Kendall, because he, like Captain Burke, saw himself as the quintessential cavalier. But his "light duty" was coming to an end. This was getting serious.

It was Josh Kendall and Billy Porter's turn to handle the dogs. The bloodhounds were the responsibility of the entire cavalry unit, but the day-to-day caring and feeding of the animals was rotated among the horse soldiers. That meant, for the most part, feeding them whatever food scraps were left over from the soldiers' supper.

Corporal Billy Porter was a twenty-one year old cavalry veteran, and didn't care a twig for the town duty he had been assigned. He relished the possibility of action. Porter was tall and somewhat heavy with close cropped brown hair. His stature was not well suited for the cavalry—short and thin was the preferred build—but his skill on a horse was unequaled. Like Kendall he was a farm boy. "Josh, let's get movin' lickety-split. I don't want Burke breathin' down our necks."

The two men saddled their horses, grabbed their canteens, carbines and sabers, if they had one—both men did—and returned to the cavalry camp. Kendall mounted his horse. He held the ropes on two of the hounds. He was very familiar and relaxed around dogs. His family had a passel of them on their farm. Porter didn't care one way or the other about the hounds. Their job was to find, attack, and kill, if necessary, their prey.

Kendall had named his two dogs Jefferson and Davis. Porter, not to be outdone, had named the hounds he held Bobby and Lee. The dogs were companion pets to the entire cavalry, but vicious animals to any deserters or draft evaders. All the troopers loved the names. So did Burke.

The weather was cold and damp. Two days earlier it had rained heavily. The day would not be a pleasant one for the squad, and the misery of the five men increased as it wore on. The horses sloshed through the mud at a slow pace. A few of the cavalrymen wore rubber ponchos, most did not. Those unfortunate ones quickly became chilled to the bone. Burke wore his poncho and made sure it completely covered his revolver and saber.

The four dogs had been released from their ropes and loved splashing through the brown sludge. Jefferson, Davis, Bobby, and Lee roamed ahead of the riders, their noses touching and smelling every blade of grass, twig, branch, or bush in their path. Logan Burke was not too hopeful his squad would find anyone—too wet for the dogs to pick up any scent, too miserable for any bushwacker to be out in this muck. But he led his patrol towards Newport as planned. Hours passed.

Burke put any idea of foraging through Newport out of his mind as soon as his squad reached the town. The hamlet was little more than a collection of small wooden buildings and shacks on both sides of a dirt road—a bughill in Burke's mind. The few outlying farms looked shabby and abandoned. The countryside was barren. War had been through here. Captain Burke halted the column only long enough to rest his men and their horses. Kendall and Porter let their hounds run free. "Go on ahead, Jeff, rustle us a quail or two," said Kendall. Billy Porter just rolled his eyes. The horses, dogs, and men were covered in mud. The air smelled of dampness. After fifteen minutes Burke resumed the patrol. They headed due east, skirting Attala County's southern border.

As the cavalrymen neared the Natchez Trace the squad picked up its pace. The soldiers knew they were about halfway through the patrol and were looking forward to getting back to Kosciusko and their camp. Josh Kendall, especially, had had enough. He was cold and wet but felt lucky no one had taken a shot at him. Billy Porter wanted more for what he was going through. After his boring duty in town, he wanted some action—some excitement—anything to show for this shitty day.

When Burke's column reached the Yockanookany River his men searched for a ford shallow enough to allow them to cross. Privates Jackson and Monroe, riding up and down the west bank, eventually found a spot near the Attala County border with Leake County. Burke's squad crossed easily, the four hounds splashing happily through the muddy water, and a couple of the horses stopping to lap up a drink. "Get movin'!" Burke yelled when he saw part of the column stalled in mid-stream. He didn't want his men exposed as they were at the Scoobachita.

The terrain on the eastern side of the river was thick with tall grass, heavy brush, and thick clustered trees. The patrol was nearing New Hope Church when the four dogs suddenly froze.

"You there! Stop where you are or I let loose the dogs!" Josh Kendall yelled. He was surprised at the sound of his own voice letting go with such a command. He saw Jefferson and Davis freeze in their tracks. They were off rope and waiting for a command to attack. Kendall had been ahead of the rest of his squad by about thirty or forty yards. He held his carbine at eye level. The rest of the patrol rounded a bend in the road and came into sight. The soldiers' guns immediately came to the ready. Porter, as much as he didn't want to, held Bobby and Lee in check. All four dogs were barking and growling. Captain Burke rode up next to Kendall, his Colt was in his hand. They were all looking directly at Lewis Bryant.

"Who are ya?" Burke demanded.

Bryant had two choices. He could either continue his charade as Calvin Wade and be treated as a suspected guerrilla—he was holding his rifle—or give his real name, which would identify him as a draft dodger. Neither choice sounded good to him, and both would result in his arrest. Lewis Bryant figured the end of the line was here and now.

"Lewis Bryant."

The name didn't mean anything to Burke. "Why're you here in these parts?"

"I'm a huntin' can't ya see?" Bryant held up his rifle, arms outstretched, hoping this would satisfy the man. He wasn't about to squeal on his new found family in the woods. If he didn't return to their camp they'd figure he had either been captured, killed, or simply decided to move on. No matter what, Bryant knew they would break camp quickly and move on.

"Monroe, take this man's rifle and tie his hands." Monroe dismounted, grabbed Bryant's squirrel gun, turned him around, and tied his hands behind his back with the rope he carried on his saddle.

"General, yer barkin' up the wrong tree. I ain't done nothin' wrong." Lewis said this in a mocking tone. He knew this officer wasn't a general, but he thought he'd needle him anyway. It was Bryant's nature.

Burke ignored the "general" reference. "There've been raids on our army patrols as well as on the citizens all across the county. I'm takin' you back to headquarters in town. They'll know what to do with ya. I'm thinkin' yer one of them guerrillas."

"Now Colonel, let's not be hasty. This is all a big misunderstandin'." Bryant dug at him again.

"Shut yer trap," yelled Burke. He was now getting irritated. Turning to the rest of his squad, he said, "Let's move out."

The ride back to town was uneventful. Burke knew he probably wouldn't snag any more runaways. He felt lucky he had captured the one he had. Maybe Massey would let up on him a bit, and not chew his ass for empty results all the time. Hell, we got the pastor, didn't we?

The cavalry patrol entered Kosciusko and rode directly to the courthouse. Captain Massey heard them approach and met them at the door.

"We got a live one, Captain," Burke said with a smile as he got down from his horse. Bryant had been ordered to walk in front of the cavalry squad followed by the four hounds. They were now back on their ropes. Still bound, Bryant now stood facing Massey. "Said his name's Lewis Bryant," Burke offered.

The name didn't mean anything to Captain Massey any more than it did to Burke. Draft records were spotty at best—some lost, others destroyed—so it wasn't surprising that Massey didn't connect Bryant's name to that of a draft evader.

"Major, I keep tellin' your Lieutenant here that this is all a big mistake." At this point Lewis Bryant didn't care who he offended. "Can't a fella go huntin' without being hassled?"

Captain Massey disregarded the ridicule. He called for Sergeant Turner and Corporal Dolan. "Lock this man in the guardhouse, but not with the Reverend. Bring him upstairs. Put him in another room under guard. I don't want the two of 'em together."

"So what's the charge, Captain?" Bryant now wanted to play it safe.

"Suspicion of guerrilla activity."

# 8

# The Disappearance

IN THE WEEKS SINCE he had been arrested the parade of visitors to the courthouse to see Reverend Sweatt continued, much to the annoyance and inconvenience of Captain Massey. Foremost among them was Margaret Sweatt.

The Reverend's wife brought him food, blankets, books from his small library at home, and a change of clothing. Lying on the floor in a pile of straw had given Nathan much pain, and his clothes looked the worse for it. She even demanded that Massey give her husband a proper bed to sleep in. Margaret's badgering of the captain paid off. He not only ordered a cot brought in for the Reverend, but even supplied soft feather bed ticking. Eventually Massey broke down and finally allowed the couple's children to visit in the courtroom along with their mother.

Margaret came almost daily. Sometimes she drove into town alone, leaving the children to work the farm by themselves, sometimes she came with her children. Many times she was accompanied by Albert Mitchell and his wife Sally.

It was during one of the family visits that Nathan had to reassure his children, once again, that all would be well. It was October 5. Almost a month had passed since the Reverend's arrest.

"Pa, when are ya comin' home?" Little Cicero looked up at his father with questioning eyes. He had climbed onto the chair next Nathan and leaned his head on his father's shoulder. "It's terrible hard on us workin' the farm by ourselves. And I miss you somethin' fierce." All of Nathan's children, along with his wife, sat around him in the courthouse gallery. Cicero, the youngest of Nathan's children, idolized his father. In his eyes his "Pa" could do no wrong. He'd trail behind his father whenever he could, asking questions about anything and everything. Nathan would usually give his son a smile at those times and rub his hand through Cicero's mop of black hair. When he wasn't able to tag along with his father, he'd follow his brother John about and become a nuisance to him. The two boys were a year apart in age.

"I don't know, son. I really don't. I wish I could give an answer, but I'm completely in the dark. They won't tell me a thing." Cicero buried his head in the folds of his father's coat. "But I'll be home again, and everything will be as it should. You be sure to help Mama and remember me in your prayers."

"You know I will. I always do." Cicero began to cry, as Nathan hugged his son even tighter.

Nathan's son John, the quiet one, sidled up to his father. He was always eager to do what was asked of him without complaint. He hoped that one day he could accompany his father and James on their trips into town. Johnny, as his father called him, would observe all about him with inquisitive eyes, always curious. When Nathan put his arm around him, John looked up at his father with searching eyes. "I know what you're thinking, Johnny. I'll be fine."

When his youngest daughter, Amanda, came to sit by her father Nathan broke into a broad grin. She may have been quiet, like her brother John, but was always ready with an encouraging word when needed. "You're comin' home soon, Poppa. I know it! Don't be sad, we'll be together soon." Amanda loved her older sisters and tried to emulate them whenever she could. She played "mother" to John and Cicero at times much to their annoyance. Nathan smiled gently and said, "I know we will, Mandy."

Mary was the Reverend's third daughter. She was short, like her mother, but with a full figure like her father. Her long raven black hair was always pulled back tightly about her head. She was the serious one and studied the Bible more than any of her brothers or sisters. When Mary took her turn sitting next to her father, all she said was, "Isaiah 40." Nathan closed his eyes and, holding Mary's hand, recited, "Comfort, oh, comfort my people, says your God." Before he could continue Mary added, "Speak tenderly to Jerusalem and tell her that her sad days are gone." Nathan smiled at his daughter, proud of her knowledge of the Scriptures. "Yes, Mary. Don't be sad," he said. As one they quietly whispered, "The Glory of the Lord will be seen by all mankind together."

Nathan's four daughters each hugged their father in turn. Easter, the oldest one, said, "Poppa, don't worry about us. We'll manage. Take care of yourself best you can, and we'll come visit every chance we get. We all love you and pray for you." Easter was tall, like her father, with curly straw-colored hair and a round face. Her kind smile and caring ways made her a second mother to the other children. With her father now gone from the family Easter would step in and take charge whenever her mother became completely overwhelmed by the family's plight.

Jen then approached her father. She whispered in his ear, "They may have you, but we have the Lord. They will never break you." Jen was a bundle of energy. Feisty, combative if need be, and always ready to defend her mother and father she was the sister who didn't give a damn what others thought or said about her family.

Nathan looked into Jen's eyes and saw his Margaret from so many years ago. He didn't trust himself to speak, so with tears welling up in his eyes he simply said, "I know," and kissed her forehead.

The last of his children to say goodbye was James. He practically jumped onto his father's lap. When the flint strikes the iron the spark produced was James. His energy was boundless and contagious. His curly unruly hair and blue eyes along with his ear-to-ear grin, gave him a mischievous and devilish appearance. Always eager to help his father with any chore he could—sometimes in competition with his brother John—James always looked forward to their trips into town. He would defend his father against anyone if he could.

"No one's gonna hurt ya, Pa. I'll make sure of it. Don't ya worry. I can handle it. I ain't afraid of any soldiers." James was just a boy, but with a man's determination.

Nathan smiled at his son's resolve, but turned serious when he said, "James, I think our family has enough on its plate the way it is right now. We don't need any more trouble than we already have. I need you to be strong, not just for me, but for your brothers and sisters, too. And most of all for your mother. They all need you at home. With William and Nathan gone you're the man of the house now. I need you to promise me you'll do good by them."

James, with downcast eyes, his enthusiasm somewhat drained, said softly, "I promise, Pa. I'll make ya proud. I will." Nathan gave him a hug. "I know you will, son, I know you will."

When Margaret came to say goodbye, Nathan took her in his arms. Neither spoke a word, but each looked the other in the eyes and smiled. Their bond of love would sustain them. She left him with the words she always would use to reassure him, "We'll get by." It was the last time Nathan Sweatt would see his family.

The townspeople never forgot the Reverend. From the time he was arrested he was visited by a collection of Kosciusko's citizens. The mayor, R.J. Mosby, was a frequent visitor, as was Jim Wallace, the circuit and chancery clerk. Jason Niles, a well known attorney in town and, like the Reverend, a strong supporter of the Union and an anti-secessionist, would call on him many times. Nathan's friend George Harlow would return often, as did John Henderson. People would bring the Reverend small cakes or corn bread, flowers, and newspapers; anything to make his incarceration bearable. Nathan Sweatt, though, spent the majority of his time quietly reading his Bible.

Nothing, however, would change the Reverend Sweatt's status as Massey's prisoner. Suspicion of guerrilla activity, he knew, was all he needed to keep the preacher locked up. No formal charges were ever lodged. Things would soon change dramatically.

It rained heavily on the morning of October 6. The sky was a dark gunmetal gray. Black clouds had formed to the east, towards Winston County, a portend of even heavier rain. It wouldn't stop John Henderson, though, from paying a visit to the courthouse. Henderson had locked his grocery and dry goods store early and quickly ran over to Captain Massey's office, his huge frame striding across the square and through Kosciusko's muddy streets. He arrived at the courthouse thoroughly drenched, his shoes and pants covered in Attala mud. Massey's office was empty. Henderson looked into the courtroom. It, too, was empty. In fact, there were no guards at all, except for the two sentries standing at the courthouse front doors.

"Where is Reverend Sweatt?" Henderson asked one of the soldiers. "Has he been discharged or removed somewhere?"

The sentry answered, "I don't know."

"Has he been taken to another location?" Henderson thought, perhaps, the cavalry camp.

"Couldn't say," was the only reply.

Henderson turned to the other sentry. "Where is Captain Massey?"

"Off on official business, I reckon."

Henderson was now both concerned and angry. "Where are the other guards?"

"Been dismissed from their posts," the first soldier answered.

With that John Henderson immediately went to George Harlow's office at the *Chronicle*. Practically bursting through the door he said, almost yelling, "Nate's missing." Harlow had been setting type. He stopped and looked up with a surprised expression.

"Sure a that?" Harlow dropped the ink covered rag he was holding.

"No question about it. The guards know nothing, or they've been told to say nothing."

"And Massey?"

"Nowhere to be found."

In a small town like Kosciusko, word spread fast. Other people trying to visit Nathan Sweatt were also faced with an empty guardhouse and tight-lipped soldiers.

When Harlow and Henderson walked outside they saw crowds gathering in small groups. Speculation and questions were rampant. People wanted to know what had happened and what, if anything, should be done about it. Should they find and confront Captain Massey for an explanation? Had the Reverend been murdered? Harlow and Henderson feared the worse. They realized the townsfolk were in a tough situation.

Any questions regarding the whereabouts of the Reverend would have to be handled carefully. No accusations could be made lest the military come down hard on the citizenry and their property. It would be a delicate balance. People feared the Confederate authorities.

A small gathering of men assembled in the post office later the same day to discuss the matter. As they collected themselves around the woodburning stove in a corner of the room, James Wallace made a suggestion. Wallace was a man of average height, but walked with a pronounced stoop, the result of a broken back from falling off his porch at the age of five. He had a head of thick white hair and wore a small white moustache.

"What say you all to a petition?" he began. "A petition to Captain Massey asking for an explanation of the Reverend's disappearance. We tell him that we know Nate's gone, and many of us fear for his life. That we ask Massey to give us some satisfaction as to what became of him. A petition signed by the citizens of our town."

"I agree," Henderson said, as he puffed on a cigar.

"Sounds reasonable," added Harlow. "Seems like the right thing to do. Maybe the only thing."

Jason Niles, standing to one side with his whiskered chin and stern face looking as though it had been chiseled in stone, wanted to know who would draw up the petition. He was, after all, a lawyer. Who better than himself, he thought.

Colonel Shelman Durham, captain of the Home Guard, however, had already been working on it. Durham, a tall lean gray haired old stick of a man, was not really a colonel. It was an honorary title. He had fought in the Black Hawk War and in the Mexican War and was present at the capture of Mexico City in 1847. He had been a private. The townspeople had bestowed the honorary rank on Durham, and he loved it.

After scribbling some notes and sentences on a piece of post office foolscap Durham presented it to the others. Each man read it in turn.

"Looks good to me," said Harlow.

"It'll do," agreed Wallace, the last one to read it. "I'll take it around town myself."

James Wallace carried the petition to all the shops and businesses in town. He made a circle of the square, poking his head in every door and stopping citizens in the streets to explain the petition and ask for signatures. Everyone who had been at the post office meeting that morning had signed. A few of the people Wallace had asked to sign said they would. But he was surprised at how many wouldn't. Those who refused to put their names on the paper gave almost the same reason why they wouldn't.

"I can't do it, Mr. Wallace," said Jonah Davis. "I got a lot to lose, here," he said as he leaned on his bar. "That Captain Massey made it pretty sure to me what he could do to me an' my tavern. This is all I got." Davis also wouldn't discount the fact that Massey spent his money here. He was good for business.

"I understand," was all Wallace could answer.

So it was with the other folks he approached who wouldn't sign. It wasn't that they weren't concerned over the Reverend's disappearance, they were oftentimes more worried over the danger to themselves and their property in making Captain Massey and his men mad at them for pressing any investigation too far. The military had little respect for the civil law or its officials. Wallace also heard from those who felt quite the opposite. Some expressed the feeling that anyone uttering disloyal sentiments ought to be summarily shot.

Wallace, his hopes dimming quickly, was about to return to the post office when he spotted two ladies walking towards him. Alleta Coleman and Fannie Bridges had just left the town's restaurant. He approached the two ladies, explained the petition, and asked for their signatures. Alleta protested immediately.

"Oh no, no, Mister Wallace. I surely can't. All I have is my little business, and if the authorities take that away I'll have nothing. I love the Reverend. I go to his services every Sunday." Alleta Coleman was a seamstress and ran her business from her home. She would repair garments, stich bonnets, sew entire dresses, or knit shawls for her customers. Her fees were nominal, but enough to keep herself out of debt. Alleta's husband had been killed at the Battle of First Manassas in 1861. "But with Efron gone it's all I got left."

Fannie Bridges was more direct with her answer. "Gimme that paper, Jim. I'll sign it right now." Fannie ran the café where the two ladies had just eaten. She and her cook, Luther, did a brisk business on most days. Luther was a free black man who she had hired the minute he walked through her restaurant's door. He had been a cook with the occupying Union army in Jackson. She paid him better wages than the army had. "I like the Reverend, too. He an' his kin have stopped in for a meal more than once. But I don't like what's been done to him. And what's that Captain Massey fella gonna do to me? Shut me down? He's a regular customer at my place. Better food than that army fodder they feed him." Fannie scribbled her name on the petition and handed it back to Wallace. "There ya go, Jim." Wallace politely thanked the women and continued his search for signatures.

After a fruitless hour of canvassing the town and gathering few signatures, Jim Wallace returned to the post office. The men who had assembled there that morning were still there when Wallace walked through the door.

"What's the good word?" asked Harlow.

"Next to nothing." Wallace held up the petition for all to see. The signatures were few. No one said a word. John Henderson broke the silence.

"We need to do something," he said, stating what everyone knew was the obvious.

"Let's go see Massey," Wallace said as he put a match to his pipe.

"All of us?" asked Harlow.

"No." It came from Colonel Durham who stood next to the stove. "He ain't gonna like a posse of us in his face."

"Makes sense," said Wallace, as he filled the room with his tobacco smoke. "Anyone here have a mind to go?"

After a short discussion it was decided that only three should visit Captain Massey. The petition was left behind.

James Wallace, George Harlow, and John Henderson—three men the town knew well—walked over to the courthouse and approached the two sentries. The rain had let up a little, but the streets were still soggy. Unlike earlier when he ran straight into Massey's office, Henderson thought the three of them should make at least some semblance of an official visit.

"We're here to see the captain," Henderson said as calmly as he could. One of the soldiers turned and walked into Massey's office. When he returned all he said was, "Go in."

Conrad Massey sat behind his desk. He was about to light a cigar when the three men came into his office, dragging mud across the floor. Wallace immediately saw the cot in the corner of the room. The same cot his friend Nate Sweatt had been given to use as his bed. Wallace felt a pit in his stomach.

"What can I do for you gentlemen?" Massey said as though he hadn't a care in the world. He glanced at their mud splattered shoes. He knew why they were there.

"Captain, we all know," Henderson began, as he gestured with his hands towards Wallace and Harlow, "that Reverend Sweatt is no longer being held here. The entire town knows. We all have suspicions and questions as to where he is, and we'd all appreciate some satisfaction in the matter."

After firing up his cigar and taking several long draws on it, Massey replied, "Well, Mr. Henderson, can't say that I blame ya. Ya see the fact of the matter is, and not that it's any of ya'll's business, I received some news a day or two ago that some bushwackers and renegades were forming up in the north county. Kinda where my cavalry was ambushed a while back. Heard it was a considerable size company of men, too. And the kicker was they were gonna march right into town and rescue the preacher." Massey paused to let his words sink in. Wallace, Harlow, and Henderson stood quietly waiting for more.

"As a consequence," Massey continued, "I sent the prisoner under guard to the jail in Carthage for safe keeping, least 'til I can send him to army headquarters." Massey looked at the three men. "That's all I can tell ya, gentlemen."

The three men looked at each other. It was as though they had just hit a brick wall.

Not knowing what to say further, Henderson simply said, "Thank you for your time, Captain." That was the signal for the three of them to leave.

Once outside Wallace said, "So what d'ya think?"

"Gotta take him at his word, I guess," Henderson said, though not really sure he believed Massey's explanation.

"Not sure we can do otherwise," added Harlow.

As word of the interview spread throughout town most everyone believed Massey's story. Some, though, had a great deal of doubt. When Jonah Davis learned of Massey's explanation, his only comment was, "Massey ain't worth a pile of owl shit. I trust him 'bout a far as I can spit. An' maybe not even that far."

# 9

# The Mail Carrier

THE RAID FROM THE north county into Kosciusko to free Reverend Sweatt never happened. Captain Massey stuck by his story, though, and repeated it to anyone who asked. The cavalry still rode about the county on its usual patrols, Captain Burke still chafing on every order from Massey.

James N. Taylor had the mail contract from Kosciusko to Carthage, in Leake County, just south of Attala. Taylor was a small firecracker of a man who was not afraid to ask a question when he felt something was just not right. His personality could be gruff and raw as sandpaper, but he usually got the answers he needed. Too old for military duty, he nevertheless thought he provided a service for both towns. He was short in stature, but strong enough to handle the bulky mail bags when needed. Taylor was a regular sight along the twenty-three mile road between Kosciusko and Carthage.

It was October 5 when James Taylor walked into the Kosciusko post office with the mail bags from Carthage. He warmed himself by the office stove. It was mid-morning. He had left Carthage at dawn.

"I see you got yourself an early start," said Seaborn Durham, the postmaster, as he struck a match to his pipe.

"Yep." As Taylor hoisted his leather pouches onto the counter he said, "Not too much this time."

"We'll keep you busy, Jim. Got a load here for Carthage." Durham looked at his watch. "Are you headed out today?"

"Might as well. Lots of daylight left. I'll get there in plenty of time."

Seaborn Durham, pipe firmly clenched between his teeth, stood hands on hips watching Taylor swing the new mail bag over his shoulder. "Need help?" Durham knew the answer.

"The hell I do!" grinned Taylor as he walked out the door. Taylor's horse was tied up in front of the post office. In one swift movement he tossed the bag over the horse's rump, untied the reins, and swung himself into the saddle. He gave a wave to Durham who stood in the office door. Taylor headed south out of town.

It was early evening when James Taylor rode into Carthage and stopped at the post office. Carthage was much smaller than Kosciusko—less than 200 people—but was the seat of Leake County and nonetheless required mail service. "Here you go, Billy," Taylor said as he handed Bill Crawford, the Carthage postmaster, the mail bag. "Anything going back?" He eyed the small canvas pouch next to Crawford.

"Very little. Should be a light trip for ya." Crawford, looking out the office window, said, "Gettin' kinda dark. Startin' to rain. Why don'tcha spend the night? There's nothin' pressin' in that bag."

"Good idea. Think I'll get me a bite to eat and grab me a bed at Sadie's." Sadie's was the local boarding house and eatery. Taylor had always stayed there when in Carthage. "Anything new since I been gone?"

"Nope. I know you love the latest news, but I don't gotta thing for ya. Been quiet here. No fights, no arguments, no thefts. Not even a trial at the courthouse."

Taylor left, disappointed he had nothing to bring back to Kosciusko but a mail bag.

Sadie Canfield's boarding house was actually her home. With a spare room behind her kitchen she was able to offer lodging and a hot meal to those traveling southwest to the capital at Jackson, south to Hattiesburg, north to Tupelo, or east into Alabama.

Sadie was a plump little woman with graying hair and a ready smile. Her husband and two sons were somewhere with Lee's army in Virginia. She hadn't heard from them in over a month. She ran her boarding house as a way to support herself while her husband and boys were gone. She had given up on trying to run their farm by herself.

"Hello, there, Jim. Good to see ya again. Hope ya brought a appetite. I got some chittlins and black-eyes cookin' on the stove."

"Smells good, Sadie. Any guests, or am I it?" Taylor walked into the kitchen and put his nose over the boiling pot.

"I'm afraid you're my only victim. Ain't had a traveler in a week." Sadie dipped a wooden spoon into the stew and tasted the soupy mixture. "Needs some salt. Wish I had some. Can't find a spec of it anywhere."

Taylor smiled. "I'm sure it'll be fine. Your meals always are. Any word from your kin?"

Sadie let a frown cross her face. "Haven't had a letter from any of 'em in weeks. Ain't from me not tryin'. Good Lord, Jim. You yourself took my letters with you to Kosy. They're to be sent to the army from there. Lord knows what became of them after that. I'm worried sick!"

Jim Taylor didn't know what to say. Once he brought the mail to Kosciusko it was out of his hands. He changed the subject. "Any news I can bring back to Attala?"

"Not a word," Sadie said as she dished out her soup into Taylor's bowl. He sat at the kitchen table and began to devour the stew. "How 'bout you?"

"Well," Taylor said after gulping a mouthful of chittlins, "the authorities have arrested our local pastor, Nathan Sweatt." He wiped his mouth with his shirtsleeve. "Seems he ran afoul of the post commander."

"What in heavens for?"

Taylor sat back in his chair. "If you hadn't heard the news there was a little skirmish up near the Reverend's home in the north county. The army couldn't round up anyone after they were ambushed, so it fell on the preacher's shoulders to be their suspect.

Guerrilla activity. They say he must a been involved somehow 'cause he don't side with Richmond." Load of crap if ya ask me. Sorry, Sadie."

"No need. I've heard worse."

"And it don't help the Reverend's case that two of his boys are evading army service." This didn't sit well with Sadie.

"Jim, I don't know this preacher fella like you do. Maybe his sons got their reasons to run. I know my boys had their reasons to enlist. Same with my man. But I don't stand in judgement of anyone. That's up to the man upstairs." Sadie pointed her thumb skyward.

Taylor let it alone. He finished his stew, looked up at Sadie, and said in a weary voice, "I'm plumb tuckered out. Been a long ride an' a long day. Think I'll turn in."

"Sure enough, Jim. Make yourself at home. You know where the bunks are. Lay yourself out. I'll have a good meal waitin' for ya in the mornin.'"

Jim Taylor got up early on October 6, had a quick breakfast of eggs, hushpuppies, and coffee—he was surprised you could even find coffee in the South these days—and returned to the post office to pick up his mail bag. It had started to rain, and he knew it would be slow going back to Kosciusko. He knew almost as many people in Carthage as he did in Kosciusko, so he decided to take his time and visit with a few folks before tackling his return trip. Maybe the rain would let up by then.

Sadie Canfield and Bill Crawford were right, Taylor thought. Nothing much had happened while he had been away. He walked as fast as he could over to the courthouse, getting drenched along the way. He wanted to chat with his friend Asa Jenkins, the Leake County Clerk. The building was an old wood structure much smaller than Attala's courthouse. He found Jenkins sitting in the clerk's office thumbing through a pile of papers. Jenkins looked up and saw Jim Taylor, water dripping from his hat, standing at the office door.

"Hey there, Jim. Haven't seen you since your last coupla trips into town. How'ya doin'?" Jenkins stood up and shook Taylor's hand. Asa Jenkins was a short thin middle aged man with a full head of gray hair. He peered through small silver wire rimmed glasses.

"Fine an' dandy, Asa. Sorry I haven't been by more. Seems every mail trip these days is urgent."

Before Taylor could ask Jenkins if he had any news to bring back to Kosciusko, Asa blurted out, "Heard your Captain Massey up there has himself a rat in a cage."

Jim Taylor was taken aback. How did news get down to Carthage so fast? Jenkins read Taylor's mind. "Army courier came through here a while back. Told us about the cavalry ambush and arrest. This preacher's been hiding his sons. Then there's this dust up near the pastor's home. An' he's a Union man to boot, I hear." Jenkins couldn't seem to get the information out fast enough. "Sounds to me like ya'll got a abolitionist locked up."

Taylor wasn't sure how or what to say to Jenkins. Asa was a full blown secessionist and an ardent supporter of the Confederate government and its "peculiar institution" of slavery.

"Well, Asa, you're right. The Reverend Sweatt is locked in the courthouse jail. Whether he had anything to do with the skirmish back in September is open to question." Taylor's gruff personality began to surface. Friend or not he wasn't about to let Jenkins run wild with the truth and alter the facts. Asa began to answer when Taylor quickly cut him off. "Asa, I know the Reverend. Known him for years. He don't lie. He don't break the law. He don't believe in killing, and he wasn't near the skirmish, either."

"What about his boys?"

"I've known his sons since they were little. They're good boys. They left Attala long before Fort Sumter was fired on. Long before this war began. Nathan Sweatt don't have any idea where they are now. That was two years ago."

"I don't cotton to disloyalty, Jim." Jenkins let his voice rise. "You can paint this picture anyway you want. But in light of our friendship I'll let it go. We just don't see it with the same eye."

Taylor was relieved their conversation on this was at a dead end. There was an awkward silence before he said, "So much for the doin's up in Attala, Asa. What's been happenin' here in Leake?" He was happy to change the subject.

"Not much excitement hereabouts. Least not like you been havin' in Kosy." Asa Jenkins also was glad to drop the thorny subject. His voice took on a softer tone. "Pretty quiet," he added. "I'd offer up a cup of coffee if I had any. Seems Sadie has a corner on it."

"Thanks anyway, Asa. I gotta get this mail bag on its way." With that Taylor shook hands with Jenkins and left.

But Jim Taylor wanted to make one last stop. He quickly ran over to the Carthage jail to see his old friend Silas Webb. If anyone had news to tell it would be the jailer. Webb lived in a small wooden shack attached to an even smaller jail cell. The cell itself had a sturdy wood door with a barred window in it, and a leaky roof. Webb's shack was his office, bedroom, and kitchen. His little stove was enough to heat the place to Webb's satisfaction.

"Hello, Silas." Taylor stood just inside the office door, trying to keep out of the rain. It didn't help. He was wet and cold.

"Good to see ya, Jim. What brings ya to Carthage?" Silas Webb was a fat little man with an unshaven face of black whiskers. He wore a brown slouch hat over his bald head. "How are ya? And Good God, come in outa this flood!" That was a tough task. Webb's office was barely large enough for his bulky frame alone. Taylor squeezed himself in anyway.

"Doin' good, Silas. I'm just here on my usual mail run. Thought I'd visit some friends while waiting out the rain. Doesn't look too good, though."

"Well, stand by my stove there. Maybe you can dry off a tad."

"Thanks." Taylor warmed his hands over the stove. The heat felt good and took some of the chill off. "I been askin' everyone I've seen if they had any news I could take back to Kosciusko. You know they love to hear the latest up there. Seems I'm their mail mouthpiece." Silas chuckled at this.

"Sorry to disappoint, Jim. Been quiet as a graveyard. Jail's been empty for a coupla days. Not even a drunk to lock up." Webb spit a wad of tobacco juice on the floor as an exclamation point.

Taylor knew that staying any longer was useless. He had delayed his trip back to Kosciusko long enough. "Silas, sorry this is so short. Gotta get goin'." With a grin on his face Taylor slapped Webb on the shoulder. "Thanks for nothin', pal."

"Safe trip, Jim."

It was still raining.

Hours later that evening, when Jim Taylor, soaked to the bone despite wearing an overcoat and poncho, pulled into town, he rode to the post office and dropped off his mail bag.

"Thanks, Jim. Anything doing down in Carthage?" Seaborn Durham said as he lit his pipe.

"Not a thing. Nothin' to tell ya."

"Did ya stop by the jail to pay your respects to the good Reverend? He's livin' there now, you know." Durham, like so many in Kosciusko, was friends with Nathan Sweatt. "Word has it that Massey sent Nate down to Carthage."

"The Carthage jail's empty, Seaborn. Saw it myself. The Reverend ain't there. Matter fact, looks like he ain't even in town."

Durham had a quizzical look on his face. "Now hold there a minute, Jim. Just this mornin' we got word up here that Reverend Sweatt was sent to Carthage. Heard tell that Captain Massey sent Nate there for his own protection." Seaborn Durham's confused look turned to concern. "Somethin' ain't right, an' it don't sound good."

Jim Taylor had brought news to back to Kosciusko after all.

The news spread fast. George Harlow had closed the *Chronicle* up for the night and wandered over to the post office to hear any latest news from Carthage. John Henderson was already there, having just locked up his dry goods shop. The news stunned them.

Jim Taylor rubbed his hand across his chin, as the four men tried to grasp what had happened to Nathan Sweatt. "Well ain't that somethin'," he said. "Hate bein' the bringer of bad news, but that's the size of it in Carthage."

"Something is definitely wrong here," said Henderson. "Where's Nate? What happened to him?"

"I'll tell ya one thing. That Captain Massey fella can sure spin a story. He's got some explainin' to do. An' I'm thinkin' right now, too," added Harlow.

It was decided that Harlow, Henderson, and Seaborn Durham would visit Massey right away, no matter how late in the evening it was. Jim Taylor would stay at the post office, minding the store, and explain to anyone who entered what he knew.

Captain Massey sat in his shirtsleeves behind his desk. His uniform coat hung from a peg on the wall behind him. He had just finished his supper and had propped his feet up when George Harlow, John Henderson, and Seaborn Durham, their clothes wet and covered in mud, walked into his office.

"Hello again, gentlemen. What can I do for ya now? I see ya brought our good postmaster along this time," said Massey as he picked some food from his teeth.

"We have it on good authority that the Reverend Nathan Sweatt is not in jail in Carthage," began Henderson.

"Mail carrier says he's not even in town there," said Durham.

George Harlow, getting angrier by the minute, blurted out, "Now see here, Massey," Harlow had dispensed with the formalities and didn't care if the captain was offended, "we want some answers now! You tell a good tale, but your ending don't stand up!"

Massey was taken aback by the editor's outburst. He gathered his thoughts together before replying.

"Now let's not lose our heads here, gentlemen," answered Massey, trying to remain calm despite this unexpected confrontation. "What I told ya this morning was true. I indeed started the preacher on his way, under guard, to Carthage. I did have second thoughts, though. I was well aware of the raid..."

"What raid?" shot back Harlow." There weren't no raid."

Massey continued, "My information said otherwise, and I weren't 'bout to take any chances. There was a possibility that the raiders could intercept my guard detail on its way to Carthage. I sent a courier with instructions countermanding my order. They were to take the prisoner directly to army headquarters, instead. It would be the only way to keep the preacher safe."

"Safe from who?" demanded Harlow, spitting the words out. "I'd say Nate weren't safe from any of ya."

"And which army headquarters," asked Seaborn Durham, "the Twentieth Regiment headquarters, or the entire army headquarters?" The Army of Tennessee could be anywhere in Georgia.

"To the Twentieth, which is with the army right now. The Reverend should be far away from here by all accounts." Massey hoped this would settle the matter. He wanted to be rid of the three men.

John Henderson and Seaborn Durham knew there was nothing more they could say or do. They were left, once again, with taking the captain's word at face value. Harlow, though, was indignant as they left Massey's office.

"What's he take us for, a bunch a fools? Now we're gettin' a total new story from just this mornin'."

"What can we do?" said Henderson. "We're back where we started." He thought for a moment. "This won't sit well with anyone."

And it didn't. Without any evidence to the contrary, the Reverend Sweatt was under guard on his way to headquarters, somewhere. No one believed it, and it was becoming a common assumption among the townspeople that Nathan Sweatt had been murdered. There were a few, though, who could only hope that Massey's statement was true. Margaret Sweatt was one of them.

# 10

# The Deep Hole

MARGARET SWEATT WAS BESIDE herself. The last time she and her children had seen the Reverend was on October 5, the day before he disappeared. She had planned to ride into town with the children in two days to bring Nathan more supplies. On the evening of October 6, however, James Wallace brought the troubling information to her door that her husband had been taken from the courthouse jail. He told Margaret of Captain Massey's explanations—both of them—and told her that no one believed either one of them. With this news Margaret insisted on calling on Massey herself. Wallace persuaded her to wait until morning. Night was creeping on and he said it might be too dangerous to hazard a trip in the dark. She didn't like it but said she would travel the next day.

In the weeks since the Reverend's arrest Margaret and the children tried to manage the farm as best they could. Margaret would work the fields with Mary, James, Amanda, John, and even Cicero. Easter and Jen remained in the house preparing meals. At times Albert Mitchell and Sally came by to help in any way they could. Margaret even kept her husband's Sunday services going despite his absence. Lacking any formal sermons the congregants took turns reading passages from the Bible, singing hymns, and praying for the Reverend's safe return. Albert Mitchell was not the best speaker nor reader, but he stumbled through his reading nevertheless.

Mitchell approached the pulpit slowly. He had little education in his youth. Most of his years had been spent in manual labor. He looked down at Sally, then at Margaret and her family. He cleared his throat and began.

"I'm lookin' at the twenty-seven Psalm here, an' it says 'The Lord is my light an' my savation; who do I feer? When avel, uh, bad men come to destraw me they're gonna fall.'" Mitchell, with Margaret's help, had chosen Psalm 27 for a reason. The good Reverend had quoted it when both men had been arrested and locked in the guardhouse. It had been a comfort to him then, it was a comfort to him now.

Margaret Sweatt, along with Albert Mitchell, rode into Kosciusko the next day. The rain had let up, and October 7 saw sunshine peaking through scattered clouds. Margaret wore a calico dress and her usual white apron. Her long black hair was held in place with a velvet mesh snood. Mitchell's wool coat had as many holes in it as his tattered hat, but it was all he had.

"I want to hear the captain tell me to my face what happened to Nathan," she said as she climbed down from the wagon.

"Might be we'll hear the same story as everyone else," Mitchell said as he followed her into the courthouse. The two of them walked right past the two guards and into Massey's office. They found Captain Massey sitting behind his desk in his shirtsleeves looking through a stack of papers. He didn't stand when she approached him.

"Captain."

Massey looked up with a disinterested look on his face. He knew who she was. "What can I do for ya today?" He knew why she was there.

"My husband was taken from this place and sent to Carthage. He never made it there. Word has it you sent him there then decided against it. I want to know where he is right now and is he safe." Margaret said this in a steady voice trying to keep her emotions in check.

Massey leaned back in his chair. "He's safe, ma'am, and under guard."

"Where is he?" Margaret had an urgency in her voice.

"He's been sent to army headquarters."

"And where's that?" she persisted.

"Mrs. Sweatt," this was the first time he had addressed her by name, "the Army of Tennessee could be anywhere in east Tennessee right now. Possibly in Georgia. General Bragg is in command. I don't tell him where to go. The army's on the move."

"When will my husband get there?" Margaret wouldn't let it go.

"There are miles 'tween here an' Chattanooga, least that's where I last heard Bragg was at," Massey said with an exasperated tone. I can't tell her what I don't know. "When I find out anything more I will be sure to inform ya." These last words Massey said with an emphasis on each one, hoping this would end the meeting with the Reverend's wife. Mitchell stood behind Margaret, hat in hand, and remained quiet. She wanted to say more, but it seemed pointless. She'd get nothing more out of the captain.

A pall of uncertainty hung over Kosciusko and the county for days and weeks. No news was coming into town about the whereabouts of the Reverend Sweatt, and Captain Massey was not forthcoming with any new information. Life would continue in Attala County, though. Births, deaths, quarrels, arrests, trials, war news, church services, farming—all the things that made life in the county what it was in 1863—never changed. Margaret Sweatt's desperation over her husband's disappearance, however, grew steadily.

November 16 dawned clear and cool. It had been 41 days since Reverend Sweatt went missing from the county courthouse. It was a Monday morning, and Caleb and Toby decided they wanted to catch their morning meal. The two black field hands, both freedmen, headed towards the Yockanookany River. Their ramshackle huts were close by each other and near the river. They lived only a mile and a half south of Kosciusko, but rarely ventured into town, and only then to sell what they caught.

Caleb and Toby were brothers. They lived on what was left of John Mackay's farm south of Kosciusko. Mackay had bought them at an auction in New Orleans back in '59. They were the last two slaves remaining on the farm. Earlier in the year, when it seemed as though a blue Yankee wave would sweep over the state following the Federal victories at Jackson and Vicksburg, most of Mackay's slaves ran off to follow the Union army, emboldened by President Lincoln's Emancipation Proclamation in January. The elderly John Mackay had no family. He was a sick and dying man. The loyalty Caleb and Toby showed by staying on to work the deteriorating farm was rewarded by Mackay granting them their freedom, their emancipation, upon his death. Whether the brothers stayed on because it kept food in their bellies, or simply because they had a fear of the unknown was anyone's guess. But they cherished their "free papers," as Caleb called them.

After Mackay's death Caleb and Toby farmed what little of the land they could. It was just the two of them now. They stayed clear of Mackay's abandoned farmhouse, preferring instead to live in the former slave cabins, the only homes the men had known for most of their entire lives. Everyone in the county left the brothers pretty much alone, some not even realizing there was anyone left on the property, and the brothers kept to themselves.

Caleb was the older of the two men. Both of them, now in their twenties, were strong and muscular from years of hard labor. They didn't know what their future held, only that they were free.

"Cabe, I knows de cats gonna be bitin'," said Toby as he shuffled his bare feet through the tall grass alongside the Yockanookany.

"If'n dats what'cha want. I gone for de bass. Dey be bitin' good a late." Caleb dropped his switch stick line into the murky water.

The Yockanookany River flowed seventy-eight miles into the Pearl River south of Kosciusko. It was more swamp than river in certain parts, slow moving and clustered with cypress trees clogging the waterway. The two men stared into the murky brown slush each hoping for a tug on his line. As Caleb and Toby sat on the riverbank the stagnant smell of decaying wood enveloped them.

After a fruitless hour the two brothers were ready to call it quits. "I tell you now, dey ain't no fun in dis," said Toby, thinking they would have to settle on turnip greens for their breakfast again.

"I speck you right, Tobe." Caleb stood up. "Les try de Deep Hole. We ain't cotch nuthin' 'round here." The Deep Hole on the Yockanookany usually produced catfish, bass, and pickerel. It was a spot in the river where the bottom fell away and provided a bountiful feeding ground for fish. Maybe along the way, Caleb thought to himself, they could catch themselves a swamp turkey.

Toby followed his brother deeper into the swamp making sure to keep an eye out for water moccasins hidden in the grasses. Trees overhanging the water and the bank blocked out the sun. Mosquitoes buzzed around their heads. The mud was soft under their feet. The brush became thicker, catching on their clothes, as they came closer to the Deep Hole. Caleb and Toby pushed their way through some chest high thickets and finally arrived at the hole.

Caleb saw it first. Something was floating on the dark water. His mind raced. "Gator!" he blurted out. "No wait." It wasn't a fallen cypress log either. No, this looked human—the clothes, the pants—all surrounding a deteriorating mass of flesh covered with flies. A large rock was tied to it.

"Les see who it be," whispered Toby. He leaned over the riverbank to get a closer look.

"Leave 'em be. We gotta tell some'um."

Toby stared at his brother. "That ain't for me, Cabe. You's askin' for trubber. You want dis laid on yo back? I'm runnin' high back home." With that Toby grabbed his pole, turned, and ran back to the Mackay farm leaving Caleb to decide what he should do.

"Tobe! Hold up!" Caleb yelled as he watched his brother thrash his way back through the thick brush and brambles. Either Toby didn't hear his brother, or didn't care, and this annoyed Cabe to no end. They weren't just brothers, they were each other's best friend. The yoke of slavery, the conditions in which they grew up, and the absence for almost their entire lives of a mother or father had forced the boys to rely on one another more and more over the years. When John Mackay bought Caleb and Toby they became separated from their parents forever. John Mackay had no interest in buying their mother and father. All they had from that point on was each other.

Caleb stood by the Deep Hole for several minutes while his mind raced through the possibilities of what he should do. The closeness of the surrounding weeds and bushes cut off any semblance of a breeze, and the murky stagnant water seemed to strangle his breath. The stench of the body and the swarming flies and mosquitoes began to make Caleb sick. His head swirled in a dizzying circle of confusing thoughts.

Cabe knew what the right thing to do would be. He and his brother had stayed out of trouble their entire lives, not once receiving a whipping from Mackay or his overseer. He knew he should report his discovery to someone in town, but he also didn't want to be connected in any way as to why or how this body ended up in the river. He also knew he could walk away right now and no one would be the wiser. The elders—the older slaves—on Mackay's farm, though, had helped to raise the brothers and taught them right from wrong.

With more trepidation than he had ever felt in his life, Caleb decided to head to Kosciusko and the sheriff's office. He pushed his way out of the dense scrub and made for the dirt road that led to town. He started to walk quickly, then broke into a trot, and finally began to run. Just as suddenly he stopped cold. What was his hurry? He didn't know who the body belonged to, and probably wouldn't have recognized it even if it hadn't been eaten away by fish. He dead, Caleb thought to himself. He ain't goin' nowhere, an' I din't do nothin' wrong. He resumed his trip into town. This time he walked slowly.

Alexander Noah was the Attala County sheriff. He had been elected in October of 1862 to serve a two year term. Noah was a tall, thin man with a pencil thin mustache, a high forehead, and receding brown hair. Ever since his election he had been caught between a rock and a rock, as he liked to say. He was the law of the county, a county occupied by the Confederate Army. Just where his jurisdiction ended and the military jurisdiction began was a fuzzy line in his mind. He wasn't about to step on the army's toes and give Captain Massey a reason to come down hard on him.

Alexander Noah was a friend of the Reverend Sweatt and was well aware of his arrest and disappearance from the courthouse. If Massey said it was a military matter, who was he to argue it? Sheriff Noah decided to limit himself to the arrest and jailing of drunks, vagrants, and thieves.

The sheriff was sitting at his desk at the town jail sucking on a thick black cigar and reading the *Chronicle*. Sometimes he gathered more information from the newspaper about what was happening in Kosciusko than he did from making his usual trips around the county.

There was a knock at his office door, then it slowly opened and a young black man walked in.

"Scuse, suh," Caleb ventured. Noah looked up from his newspaper. "Name's Caleb, suh,"

"I recognize you. Ya live out by the Mackay farm, right?"

"Yas suh. Me an' my brother Toby."

"What'cha doin' in Kosy? Sellin' your catch?"

"No suh. We's fishin' in de Yock an' I finds somethin'. It look like a body."

Sheriff Noah dropped his paper and sat straight up in his chair. "Where?"

"At de Deep Hole, suh." Noah knew where it was. He had fished there as a boy. He grabbed his hat and headed for the door. As he left his office and headed towards the courthouse he said to Caleb over his shoulder, "Follow me."

The two men quickly walked to the courthouse. As they crossed the square Noah turned to Caleb and told him to repeat his story to the captain. The two sentries at the courthouse door recognized the sheriff and let him pass. They eyed Caleb suspiciously.

Captain Massey had been talking to Jason Niles and Jim Wallace in his office when Sheriff Noah and Caleb walked in. Their conversation stopped, and all three turned and stared at Noah and the black man.

When Cabe walked into Massey's office and saw the three men standing there—one of them wearing a Confederate uniform—he wanted to turn and run. He didn't know who they were. The army had pretty much left Mackay's farm alone, so the only time he might have come across any soldiers would have been during his few trips into town to sell his catch. And those men ignored Toby and Caleb.

After he was told to do so by Sheriff Noah, Caleb repeated his story to Captain Massey. "Do you know who it is?" asked Massey, staring straight into Caleb's eyes.

"No suh. Don't rec'nize him one bit. He don't look like much a anythin' seems to me."

"You an' your brother, this the first time you ever saw the body?" Massey wouldn't take his eyes off Caleb.

"Yas suh." Cabe wouldn't say more.

"You boys fish the Hole a lot?"

"Yas suh. Me an' Tobe go there sum times."

"And this is the first time you spotted the body?" Caleb began to feel uncomfortable. Ah tole him all ah know, he said to himself. Ah got nothin' to do wit dis.

"Yas suh, Fust time. We only go there sum times," he said again.

Captain Massey finally took his eyes off Caleb and turned to Niles, Wallace, and Noah. The look he gave the three men said what they were all thinking.

He turned to face Caleb again. "Boy, can you take us to where you found this body?"

"Yas suh." Caleb was nervous. This was beyond anything he wanted to do, but no one, so far, had made any implication that he was involved in the appearance of a body in the river.

"Sergeant Turner!" Duncan Turner poked in around the door. "Tell Captain Burke to bring a small detail of men here at once. And bring the company wagon and two fence rails." Massey looked at the faces around him. "Ya'll can come along if ya want." Everyone there feared what they might find.

When the wagon arrived at the courthouse Massey climbed onto the bench seat next to Turner, who held the reins. Jason Niles, Jim Wallace and Sheriff Noah sat in the wagon bed with Caleb, who moved as far back in the wagon as he could. Burke and the three-man cavalry detachment followed the wagon on horseback.

It was tough going trying to get the company wagon through the mud and thick brush, and as close to the Deep Hole as possible without the bank giving way. After hacking their way slowly, sometimes with Burke's men on foot trying to clear the way, they arrived at the hole. They had stopped the wagon a few yards back and walked the rest of the way on foot.

"Here?" Massey asked Caleb.

"Yas suh. Dis is it." He wanted to be anywhere but here.

Massey leaned forward and took one look at the body and the stone tied on top of it. "Let's bring it up. You can go now, boy," Massey said without even looking at Caleb. That was all Caleb wanted to hear. He ran as fast as he could back home.

Captain Burke ordered the three cavalry troopers to guide the body closer to shore using the fence rails. When it was close enough to the riverbank they carefully hauled it up and laid it on a blanket.

Jason Niles and James Wallace took a long look at the body. So did Burke and Noah. They knew who it was. So did Massey. "Christ Almighty," he muttered under his breath. Even in its deteriorated condition he knew. "Take him to Doc Lewis"

One of the soldiers asked, "The rock, too?"

"Yeah." Massey paused, then added, "The rock, too."

They had found the Reverend Sweatt.

# 11

# The Inquest

WHEN MARGARET SWEATT LEARNED that her husband had been found, dead, her world collapsed. So many days had passed since he was last seen by anyone that she actually held a sliver of hope that he was still alive. Now that hope was gone.

Margaret and Nathan had married in South Carolina. Nathan knew of her ancestry, but he didn't care. The rumors that she was of Cherokee descent didn't bother him. She had found the man who she knew would take care of her, the man who would shield her from the taunts and barbs of those who looked down on her. She could now look forward to a life, a family, and a future of hope. Margaret knew she would support her husband in anything he chose to do. She followed his ministry and helped him grow his congregation. Before Nathan built his little church, and his Sunday services were held in the open, outside their home and under the large magnolia, Margaret would serve lemonade to the congregants after the last hymn was sung. She was now forty-eight years old, with a family of seven to feed and look after. Her hope for the future dimmed and now seemed bleak.

Albert and Sally Mitchell accompanied Margaret into town. She wanted to see her husband one final time, and no one could persuade her otherwise. She asked that the children stay at home. Easter and Jen would look after them. A small crowd had gathered outside the doctor's office. Margaret rushed past them without saying a word. She held a small handkerchief to her eyes. Albert and Sally walked on either side of her, gently holding her by the arm.

Doctor Charles Betts Galloway took Margaret's hand in his. He was a tall man with a full black beard and thick hair. "I'm terribly sorry, Margaret. This is not the ending any of us had hoped for. Nathan was a good and decent man. He deserved better than this." Margaret dabbed at her eyes and nodded her head. Galloway added, "If there's anything I can do . . ."

Margaret simply said in a quiet voice, "I would like to see him."

"I don't think that's a good idea."

"I want to see him," she said emphatically. "Now."

Galloway turned and, holding her by her elbow, led her into an adjoining room, closing the door behind them. Albert and Sally remained behind.

Doctor Ozias Lewis stood behind a long table. A gray wool blanket covered something on top of it. A large rock and length of rope lay on the floor in the corner. Lewis saw Margaret glance at it. He quickly tried to position himself in a way to block her view. He was unsuccessful. She saw it. She understood. Ozias Lewis, thin in build and short in height, stood coatless with his sleeves rolled up and his vest open. The room smelled of damp wool and something else. Something awful.

"I would like to see my husband," Margaret said. Galloway still gently held her by her elbow.

"Mrs. Sweatt," Lewis said, "Are you sure? I don't think..."

"Please. Now!"

"I must warn you that this will not look good," Lewis warned in a low voice. Margaret didn't answer the doctor but gave him a direct stare.

Lewis pulled back the blanket just far enough to reveal the head. Margaret let her breath out in a small but audible gasp. She saw the large, smooth head and wisp of gray hair. Much of the Reverend's face had been sloughed away from exposure to the river, but she saw enough to know it was him. For the rest of her life Margaret would block this memory from her mind. He would always and only be the father, the pastor, and the husband she'd known for almost her entire life.

"Thank you," she said softly as Doctor Lewis replaced the blanket. Doctor Galloway led her back to the office. "There's to be an inquest, Margaret. Mayor Mosby is acting as coroner. We want to get to the bottom of this. What happened, and who is responsible."

Margaret simply nodded her head. It didn't matter. Nothing would bring Nathan back. Let them have their inquest, their hearing. Albert and Sally helped her back to the wagon, and they returned home. Home, Margaret thought to herself. Our home, our children. Nothing will ever be the same. And our two oldest boys. They don't even know.

The ride back to Liberty was a quiet one. The only sounds heard were the creaking of the wagon's wheels and the screeching caw of a distant crow. Finally Albert Mitchell said, "He's in a better place now. He's with the Lord."

The following day, when Mayor Mosby convened the inquest into the death of the Reverend Nathan Sweatt, there was no end to the number of people who wanted to be sworn in as jurists. Mosby accepted this fact but was somewhat disgusted that several of the townsfolk who showed interest were the very same ones who refused to sign the petition to Captain Massey asking for an explanation of the Reverend's disappearance.

R.J. Mosby stood a ramrod straight five feet, five inches in height. He was a rotund man with a balding head and a huge bushy mustache. He had a habit of twirling his watch chain around his finger in circles as he talked to people. His first order of business was to swear in a jury. Wanting to be as impartial as possible he looked to select men who seemed to be unaffected by the Reverend's disappearance and death. This posed a problem for Mosby. Almost everyone he interviewed thought the army in general and Massey in particular were responsible for Nathan Sweatt's murder.

Mosby pared the group of possible jurists down to six. He settled on James Wallace, the Chancery Clerk, as the foreman. Alexander Noah, Attala's sheriff, was selected; a good choice as Mosby told himself. Thomas Sallis was Clerk of the Probate Court, and William Overstreet was the Constable of Beat 3; two more good ones, Mosby convinced himself. He selected John Holland, who was the Attala County Surveyor. He was young, and probably not as familiar with the Reverend as the other jurists. Mosby's final choice was John Hight. He was not involved in county government but was a well known citizen of Kosciusko. Hight liked to refer to himself as a "citizen at large." Was it an impartial jury? Mosby asked himself. Probably not. But all six men would be sworn to examine the case based on the facts at hand. What more could he do?

The courtroom was packed on the first day of the hearing. Smoke from dozens of pipes and cigars choked the air with a thick white cloud. Captain Massey maintained his guards at the courthouse front doors to assure order and safety. His adjacent office to the courtroom became his refuge from the proceedings. At least until the day when he would be ordered to testify. As the post commander in Kosciusko, and on military duty, he could refuse. Massey knew that would be a poor decision on his part. He was feeling the heat from this entire affair, and a refusal would have looked extremely bad.

Mosby wanted the hearing to unfold in a methodical and chronological order. He knew the eyes of the town were focused on him and how he ran this inquest. He sat at the judge's bench and twirled his watch furiously. First things first, he thought. Let's bring up the doctors. All would be sworn in.

Doctors Ozias Lewis and Charles Galloway each testified in turn. Each man gave his opinion based on his examination of Nathan Sweatt's body. Their findings were identical.

"From what we can tell," Doctor Lewis said in his slow southern drawl, "the good Reverend was hung by the neck. There was enough evidence left, even given the state the body was in, to determine that this was the case. That was the cause of death, not drowning." Mayor Mosby again twirled his pocket watch, this time popping it open every time it came to a stop at the end of his finger. "And the rock?" he asked.

"The rock weighed thirty pounds. As we all know Reverend Sweatt was quite a large man. The rock, we can assume, was meant to hold his body to the bottom of the river." Doctor Lewis paused hoping this would be the end of the questioning. It wasn't.

Like a school boy eager for a gory explanation, Mosby asked for more. "Why was he floatin' on the water?"

"Well," Lewis began, "the body's natural gasses and fluids will expand and bloat the organs causing the body, in this instance, to rise in the water. It'd take more than a thirty pound stone to hold it to the bottom."

Satisfied, Mosby said, "Thank you, Doctor. You're excused."

Mary Sweatt sat in the back of the courtroom gallery with Albert and Sally Mitchell. She rose to leave. "I've heard enough," she whispered to Albert. Just then Mayor Mosby announced, "The bench calls Captain C.K. Massey to the stand." Mary immediately sat back down.

Captain Massey sat in his office playing a game of euchre with Logan Burke. When he heard his name called he dropped his cards, stood up, and donned his kepi. He left his sword belt and revolver with Burke. Massey didn't want to appear too warlike. As he walked into the courtroom he turned to look back at Burke, who was about to return to his camp. "Stay here. That's an order." Logan Burke was irritated to no end by this.

Massey sat in the witness chair and quickly looked over at the jury box. He recognized everyone there. He also noticed that none of the men had pencil or paper. No one took notes.

"Captain Massey, did you order the removal of Nathan Sweatt from this courthouse jail?" Mosby asked in the most officious tone he could muster.

"Yes, I did," Massey said in a firm voice. "I did this for his safety and for the town's safety."

"The town's safety?"

"I had information that there might be a raid into Kosciusko for the purpose of freeing my prisoner. This coulda led to bloodshed for both my men and the town's citizens, not to mention the pastor. So I had him sent under guard to the jail in Carthage."

"And why, Captain, was the Reverend being held in the first place?" The mayor wanted to stick this in the court record even though it had nothing to do with the reason for the hearing.

"Suspicion of guerrilla activity and hiding his sons from military service in the Confederate States Army." This prompted loud groans from the gallery.

"Why did the Reverend never make it to Carthage?" Mosby asked pointedly.

"Well, I changed my mind. Figured the prisoner would be safer at army headquarters. I sent one of my men to catch the guard detail an' turn it around."

"And did they turn around?" Mosby again asked the pointed question.

"I received no information to the contrary. So I supposed they had." Captain Massey said this with a clear conscience. He had believed it true until the Reverend's body was discovered. His courier had returned, telling Massey that his order had been delivered to the escort detail.

"Who were your men escorting Nathan Sweatt?"

"It was a cavalry detail of Captain Burke's men. I don't know who he chose for the escort. Don't know their names either."

"Captain, you may stand down...for now," Mosby ordered. "I want to talk to this Burke fella. Bring him in."

Upon hearing his name called Logan Burke walked from Massey's office and took the witness stand. He left his cavalry saber and revolver in the office. He wore his bullet riddled uniform coat if for no other reason than to show all those present the danger his men faced.

Mayor Mosby wasted no time. "Captain Burke, who were the men you assigned to accompany Reverend Sweatt to Carthage? What're their names?"

"I ordered Privates Howard, Ford, Cox, and Morgan to be the guard detail." Burke said this matter-of-factly, as though it were known to everyone.

Massey, sitting in the first row of the gallery, let out an audible sigh and shook his head. Four of the six cavalry troopers who were ambushed and wounded at the Scoobachita had been assigned to guard the Reverend. What had Burke been thinking? That was a powder keg, and it had just exploded. Revenge would have been reason enough for those men to kill the pastor.

"I'd like to see those soldiers, Captain. I'm issuin' a subpoena for their appearance before this court." Mosby slammed his gavel on the bench, and added, "Court's adjourned 'til tomorrow at nine am."

Burke and Massey huddled together in Massey's small office. "Find those men, Captain. Find 'em now. We need to be as official as possible, here. We gotta be level straight." Massey wouldn't mince words. "They know what happened."

On his way out of the courthouse Burke grabbed Duncan Turner and Jimmy Dolan. "You two, yer comin' with me."

The three men hurried down to the cavalry camp. "Round up Cox, Howard, Morgan, and Ford. On my orders have them assemble at the courthouse tomorrow at nine." Captain Burke, like Massey, wanted to cooperate with the inquest. He, too, knew any refusal to do so would cast doubt on whatever he said or did.

Burke couldn't have cared less about the Reverend Sweatt. He was convinced the pastor was somehow involved in the ambush of his squad. The pastor deserved whatever he got. But the captain knew he had to ride this horse to the finish.

As Sergeant Turner and Corporal Dolan followed Burke toward the camp, the captain turned to the two men and said, "Sergeant, go tent-by-tent. I want those troopers found. Grab some other men if you need help. Corporal, you come with me. We're searchin' through town." Burke grabbed Dolan by the arm and headed to one side of the town square. "I'll start at the post office, you start at the *Chronicle* office. We'll meet at Henderson's Store. Those four may or may not be in town, but we're gonna find out." With that the two men headed in opposite directions.

Jimmy Dolan didn't know what he'd say to the cavalrymen, if he even spotted them. He knew something big was brewing inside the courthouse, and finding Cox, Howard, Morgan, and Ford had something to do with it. He didn't like the idea of being in the middle of a possible explosive situation, so he figured his best bet was to relay Captain Burke's message and consider his job done. Likely as not most townspeople he ran across wouldn't know those four men from anyone else in Company D. He wouldn't bother with them. He would do as little as he could to follow Burke's order.

Corporal Dolan found the newspaper office closed. He figured the editor, much like many of Kosciusko's citizens, was at the courthouse. He poked his head into Johnson's Harness and Leather Goods Store. Again, nothing…just a couple of farmers looking over some stirrups and a girth. Dolan was content with this. The further he could stay away from any confrontation with the troopers, the better. He went on poking his head into every store he came to. Nothing but curious stares looking back at him.

When he arrived at Davis's Tavern he lingered, then walked inside. It was the first time he had been there since he and Duncan had tracked down Captain Massey weeks ago.

Jonah Davis looked up at Dolan from behind the bar. One person sat alone at the small table in the middle of the saloon. Although it was obvious there were no troopers in the tavern Dolan figured he would ask the question anyway. But before he could, Davis said, "Soldier, hope you're not here for a sip. Can't do it. I'd be in a bucket of trouble if I served ya one."

Jimmy Dolan would've loved a glass of whiskey. He licked his lips. The tavern reeked of liquor. "Uh, no sir. Just wonderin' if any of our men been in here lately?"

Davis chuckled. "No, not a one. My best customer been your Captain Massey. He's a regular."

Dolan looked longingly at the shelves of bottles lining the wall behind the bar. He took a last look at Davis and walked out. When he arrived at Henderson's Grocery Captain Burke was waiting for him.

"Anything?" Burke asked. Dolan was, and always had been, cowed by the captain.

"No sir. And I looked everywhere. Everywhere," he added, punching the word out. He figured Captain Burke didn't believe him anyway.

"Did you talk to the locals?"

The lie came easily. "Yes sir. Everyone I met."

"Very well. Let's head back to camp."

Josh Kendall had just dozed off inside the dog tent he shared with Billy Porter when he felt a tap on his boot. He looked up and saw Porter standing outside looking down at him.

"What in hell's your problem, Billy? I ain't got no duty today. Lemme alone."

"Get up," Porter said. "We got company."

Kendall crawled out of his shelter and stood looking at Corporal Porter. Before he could say anything more, he noticed Duncan Turner standing to one side. The dogs Jeff, Davis, Bobby, and Lee were sleeping quietly next to Kendall's tent...something Josh envied at the moment.

"We gotta find Cox, Morgan, Ford, and Howard, and we gotta do it quick. Burke's on his way," announced Turner.

"What the hell for?" Kendall wanted to know.

"Don't matter. Just do it. There'll be hell to pay if we don't," said Turner. "Cap'n Burke ain't too happy."

Kendall, Porter, and Turner began to spread out among the tents in camp asking every soldier they met what they knew or saw. Jackson and Monroe, the other two cavalrymen from Burke's earlier patrol, were the first they questioned. Their pup tent was close by Kendall and Porter's. Neither soldier had any idea where the four horsemen were. "Ain't seen any of 'em," Monroe offered. "Not a one," added Jackson.

Turner had wandered down to the post hospital tent and took a look inside. It was empty. Not a sawbones nor a patient in sight. When he returned to Kendall and Porter's tent, Logan Burke and Jimmy Dolan were there. Burke's temper was slowly burning.

"What did you find?" he asked, barely suppressing his anger.

The five soldiers stood silent, looking at each other with dumbfounded expressions on their faces.

"Well?" demanded Burke.

Turner finally spoke. "Cap'n, we got nothin'. Wherever those fellas are, it ain't here."

"Me and the corporal here," Burke said, not even looking at Dolan, "checked the stables on our way over. Seems we got some horses missing." Burke was looking each man in the face one by one. "Keep searching. I want them found. Start looking beyond the town. They might be holed up in some hollow or scrub somewhere. I don't care if it takes you all night."

Burke's men knew it would be a fruitless effort, but they continued their search anyway.

Logan Burke felt a tightening in his throat, and a pit in his stomach.

At 9 o'clock the next morning Captain Burke, Sergeant Turner, and Corporal Dolan gathered in Massey's office. The three men looked as though they had lost something of great value. The gloom on their faces said it all.

"They're gone," Burke announced.

"Whatd'ya mean 'gone'?" Massey said.

"Nowhere to be found. Not in camp, not in town. We spent a good part of the night lookin' for 'em. Even turned out some of my men to help."

Massey looked at Turner and Dolan. Turner, without being asked, said, "It's true, Captain. Seems they skedaddled."

"Private Douglass is missing, also," added Burke. "Looks like the entire squad I took on patrol to the Scoobachita is missing. Even Kirkland. He was recoverin' at the post hospital, but he's gone now, too."

"Deserters," Massey said more to himself than to anyone else.

"It would seem so," Burke agreed. "They're more n' likely clear out of the county by now. Took all their gear with 'em. Even their horses, damnit!"

When this news was brought to the attention of R.J. Mosby, the mayor almost flipped his pocket watch completely off his finger. "Seems we're somewhat at a standstill here. I'm goin' to reconvene the hearin' anyway." Mosby was standing in Massey's office talking to Captain Massey and Captain Burke. The two officers stood silent. "We're gonna get through this thing somehow." With that the mayor entered the courtroom and took his place at the bench. The gallery was already packed with spectators.

One of Massey's sentries, acting as bailiff, handed Mosby a piece of paper. Jason Niles had slipped a note to the mayor asking if he could testify. He had some information of interest. Mosby announced, "It seems this court, rather the military, can't produce the soldiers in question who were guardin' Reverend Sweatt on the night of his disappearance. This is very troublin'. Be that as it may, we will proceed with this inquest. The court calls Jason Niles to the stand." The gallery erupted with surprise. Niles slowly took his place before the bench and sat down.

Jason Niles was born in Vermont, studied law there, then moved to Mississippi in the 1840's. He became a prominent citizen in Kosciusko. Although he was a strong supporter of the Union, he kept a low public profile hoping this would keep him away from the eyes of Confederate authorities. At fifty-nine years old, though, he thought he was beyond the age for military service.

"Do you have anything you could add to these proceedin's, Mr. Niles?" Mosby asked.

"Yes. I don't know if this will help matters any, but I spoke with Lewis Bryant the night after the Reverend Sweatt's disappearance." Bryant at one time was in custody by the military for alleged complicity with bushwackers. "I figured since he and the Reverend had been jailed in this very courthouse at the same time he might could shed some light on what happened to the Reverend. He informed me that there was no doubt that Nathan Sweatt had been hung the night previous. He even said that the Reverend had been taken out once before and was threatened terribly by being choked. He said that this was done in back of a graveyard, too. Bryant said that a rope was tied around the Reverend's neck and he was drawn up several times. He told me the Reverend asked if they intended to kill him. Those that took him said they intended to let him kill himself. Bryant said Nathan was led out of this courthouse at about 10 or 11 o'clock the night he disappeared."

Jason Niles took a deep breath. "Some say he was left hanging on a beech tree limb about a mile and a half down in the Yocka-nookany Swamp." Niles paused again, then added, "Don't know if what I was told is true, or whether this Bryant can be trusted. This fella's a bragger and a blowhard. Likes to puff himself up a might to make himself look important. I don't think he knows when the truth ends, and his lies begin. But there you have it. My guess is those cavalry boys did it."

The entire courtroom was stunned silent, then broke loose with an explosion of yells and commotion. Mayor Mosby stopped twirling his watch. He wasn't sure what to say. Jason Niles, having said his piece, sat quietly with his hands folded. Captain Massey was taken completely aback, as was Captain Burke. It sounded as though their entire command might have been complicit, yet no names could be attached to anyone.

Mosby immediately hit his gavel over and over. "The jury will disregard that last statement by Mr. Niles. It is pure speculation!"

Margaret Sweatt, along with the Mitchells, sat through the second day of testimony. This time she had heard enough.

# 12

# The Verdict

MAYOR MOSBY SAT AT the judge's bench collecting his thoughts. After hearing the testimony from Jason Niles, second hand as it was, he didn't want anymore surprises. Turning to Captain Massey, who was sitting in the first row of the gallery, Mosby said, "Captain, I think it would help this court if you could bring Lewis Bryant before it so we might examine him ourselves. We gotta find the truth and see what sticks to it."

Massey was now in a terrible fix of his own making. He didn't have enough on Bryant to make a case of it. Bryant had been released shortly after the Reverend had been sent on his way to Carthage. Massey stood and cleared his throat. "Lewis Bryant is no longer in custody." Commotion again broke out in the gallery.

"Now hold on a second, there, Captain." Mosby wanted to pursue this to its conclusion. "Where is he, and can ya produce him?"

Massey, red faced, said, "I'm afraid not. He disappeared into the woods where we found him originally. He knows this land well. We'd be lucky to catch him again."

Mayor Mosby realized this was a dead end. He figured it was time to wrap the proceedings up. "Does anyone have anything further they'd like to add to this hearin'?" He hoped there wasn't. After a minute's pause he turned to the jury.

THE VERDICT

"Upon no further testimony presented, the jury may now re-
tire to deliberate. This court is adjourned 'til a verdict is reached."
Mosby cracked his gavel down on the bench. He thought he had
run the inquest quite well.

The six men filed off into the jury room. The courtroom began to empty, and Captains Massey and Burke walked silently back
into Massey's office.

"This ain't my dance, Burke. Ain't yours neither. I told the
court what I knew and what I did. It was your boys who last saw the
preacher. My courier delivered my order to your men an' returned
here. What in hell were ya thinkin' assignin' those four troopers to
guard Sweatt?" Massey was hot yet kept his voice low. "Ya think
them boys weren't lookin' for some payback? A little revenge?"

Logan Burke just about had enough. "Captain, you ordered
a guard detail for the prisoner." Burke kept his voice steady and in
check, his blue eyes piercing through Massey. "You never said who
it should be. That was left to me." Burke knew the Reverend's fate
would be in the hands of his men, and he didn't care. There was always the possibility something like this might happen. In the back
of Logan Burke's mind he hoped it would. But for me personally,
he reminded himself, my hands are clean. They wouldn't dare do
anything to the military.

Massey, in a calmer voice, said, "I think we stand on firm
ground here, Captain. Matter of fact those six men of yours de-
sertin' might be the best thing that coulda happened. Looks like
they're the ones this thing oughta be pinned on." Burke nodded
his head in agreement.

When Margaret Sweatt returned to her home the children
immediately gathered around and peppered her with questions.
They knew their mother had visited Doctor Lewis and Galloway's
office. Margaret had spared them any description of their father.
They had been devastated when the Reverend's body had been
found. The finality of it all, after weeks of waiting, was too much to

bear. Margaret also explained the inquest proceedings as best she could, avoiding the details of Jason Niles's testimony.

"Will you go back for the verdict?" James asked, hoping if she did he could go with her.

"Children, I'm done in. I don't think I can handle anything more. My plate is full of grief. It won't handle more." Margaret's voice was low and weary. She drew her words out slowly. "What those men find, what they say, it won't matter. Your father is gone." Tears welled up in her eyes. "I know he would want us to keep going. And we can. With God's help we will." She had gladly accepted the offer from Albert and Sally Mitchell for their help in managing the farm. "And we must keep your father's ministry alive. It was his rock."

Margaret gathered the family around the hearth, just as they had gathered two years ago. But now it was different. Now her husband and two sons were missing from the circle. "Everyone join hands," she said softly. With closed eyes and a bowed head she spoke from memory. "Let not your heart be troubled. You are trusting God, now trust in me. There are many homes up there where my Father lives, and I am going to prepare them for your coming. When everything is ready, then I will come and get you, so you can always be with me where I am. If this weren't so, I would tell you plainly. And you know where I am going and how to get there."

"Gentlemen, what say you all?" James Wallace asked the question of the other five jurors. They had filed into the jury room one by one. It was a small room just off from the judge's bench. It held a long wood table and a smattering of twelve wooden chairs. Two oil lamps were mounted on the wall on either side of the room's single window. John Hight pulled a cigar from his coat and struck a match to it. Sheriff Alexander Noah, seeing this, pulled one from his vest pocket and did the same.

"Sure seems them soldiers in the cavalry guard were involved," Noah ventured. "I rode out a few times with the cav. There were people out in the woods what took pot shots at us. Those horse fellas have a long memory." He exhaled a cloud of white smoke. "Let's be honest, here," the sheriff said, punctuating each word by waving his cigar at the other men around the table, "all fingers are pointin' right at those boys in the prisoner escort. I'd say it's pretty obvious." He sat back in his chair, figuring he had made his case.

"Don't mean nothin'," said Bill Overstreet, a heavyset bald-headed man with a couple of chins. "Got any witnesses? Hell no. Only witnesses were them that did it, assumin' they did the murder. And they're gone." Overstreet's job as a town constable, as he saw it, was to patrol Kosciusko, apprehend, arrest, and detain any thieves or vagrants, and deliver them to Sheriff Noah at the jail. He did this as best he could, all while staying clear of Captain Massey and any Confederate authorities, a headache he didn't need. Let the military do their job, leave me alone, and I'll do mine. This was his way of thinking from the day the army first settled into town. His immense weight, though, all but precluded him from running down a criminal in a prolonged pursuit. But when caught, that suspect would've felt the full weight of the law. William Overstreet always got a chuckle out of this whenever he thought of it. He knew Nathan Sweatt and was always cordial to him whenever they met in town. The Reverend's disappearance and murder seemed to be a military matter, but the pastor was a civilian. Overstreet felt he owed it to the man to get to the bottom of all this. He added, "I wish I knew."

Thomas Sallis chimed in. "So we're left with the second hand testimony from Niles, which, I might add, came from this Bry-ant fellow. He's probably one of those bushwackers himself." Sallis, the Probate Court Clerk, was a short little man with black beady eyes that shifted everywhere. He was well spoken, having gone to school in Oxford at the University of Mississippi. "It would seem to me that we're at loose ends here. Perhaps the soldiers abandoned the Reverend, and the murder was committed by citizens, by our own townsfolk, loyal to Richmond."

"What in hell are you tellin' us, Tom?" Jim Wallace had a shocked look on his face.

"Look, all I'm sayin' is this. Not everyone in this town, or the county for that matter, is a friend of Nathan Sweatt. There's plenty of folks who just don't take to his way of thinkin'. I'll betcha there's more'n a few around here would call him a traitor. Count the signatures on that petition of yours, Jim. Sure, I signed it. I'll bet everyone at this table did, too. That's not the problem. It's the folks who didn't sign, for whatever reason, that tells the tale. Did they refuse to sign outa fear of Massey? Or was there something more?" Sallis paused, then said almost apologetically, "There might even be folks who are glad he's gone." At this the room fell silent.

John Holland, the county surveyor, had been sitting silent, listening to the discussion. "Not likely." Those were his only two words. Holland, all of twenty-four years old and fresh from college, was new to the surveyor's job. His tousled blond hair made him look closer to nineteen.

"Would you like to explain yourself?" asked Wallace.

Holland was a man short on words. "Nothing but theories and guesses," he said.

"So what're ya tellin' us, Holland?" Overstreet wanted to know.

"That we just don't know," said Holland. John Holland knew he was the most impartial juror in the room. He was too new to Kosciusko to have formed any lasting friendships yet. He hadn't even come into contact with many of the town's citizens unless it was through his work. He had heard the Reverend's name mentioned in passing conversation but had never met him. Holland was a Baptist, so his small circle of friends revolved around his church. But most important to John Holland was that he dealt in absolutes. His surveying job demanded it. All he saw were the facts before him and nothing else. "We just don't know," he repeated, this time putting weight on each word.

John Hight, still puffing away on his cigar, a long ash hanging from the end of it, finally spoke. "I don't think the damn army has done enough to get to the bottom of this thing." Hight had short black hair and a close cut black beard. He was a barrel-chested man who was gruff with anyone who disagreed with him. "Look here, now. You got this Massey fellow who plays innocent to just about everything that's happened from the day the Reverend disappeared to the day he's fished out of the Yock. According to him he don't know a thing. Then we have that cavalry pretty boy who tells us that all he did was assign the guard detail. Oh sure, the guard detail the likes of which would just as soon cut the Reverend's throat than hang him."

Hight paused long enough to flick the ash from his cigar, produce a huge cough, and shoot a wad of spit towards the cuspidor at his feet. "Did this Captain Burke even try to go after these deserters of his?" Hight asked no one in particular. "Did he try to find 'em? What if there were others in his command who were involved? And did Massey even question the courthouse guards who were on duty the night the pastor was taken?" Hight scratched his beard, lost in thought. "No, there's too many unanswered questions to my likin' for sure."

Even though Mayor Mosby had told the jurors to disregard the opinion from Jason Niles that the cavalry had killed Nathan Sweatt, John Hight wasn't about to. He had been a longtime friend of the Reverend's and, at least in his eyes, the facts were indisputable. The whole damn army, as far as he was concerned, was guilty of murder.

The room fell silent again, each man framing his opinion of the events in his own mind.

"Well gentlemen," Wallace said at last, "we have to produce a verdict for the court. As for myself, I just don't see enough solid evidence to say who did this to Reverend Sweatt. We're left with guesses and conjecture. I say we tell the court that we accept the findings of Doctors Lewis and Galloway, but we cannot come to any conclusion as to who killed Nathan Sweatt. Do we agree on this? And do we all sign the verdict as such?" Jim Wallace polled the table.

"Sheriff?"

Noah let out a long sigh. "Yes. I agree," he said reluctantly, not too sure, now, about his previous statement.

"Mr. Sallis?"

"Agreed," said Sallis as he darted his eyes at the other jurors. He didn't know what or who to believe at this point. Best to play it safe.

"Mr. Overstreet?"

Overstreet shifted his huge frame in his chair. "I'll sign." Overstreet wanted justice served, but they had no suspects in custody and no idea where to turn next.

"Mr. Holland, do you agree?" Wallace asked.

John Holland gave a simple, "Yep." The surveyor was quite confident in his answer.

"And Mr. Hight?"

John Hight fidgeted in his chair and tossed his dead cigar into the spittoon.

"No, I'm afraid not. Can't sign, won't sign."

Wallace looked at the others. "Well," he said, "this isn't a murder trial. There's no defendant. We're just voting on accepting the evidence as given." He paused before going on. "Or rejecting it. We don't have to be unanimous."

Hight looked at the others around the table. "Ya'll can sign the verdict as you see fit. Ain't gonna be me, though. If you please, Mr. Wallace, I would like to write my own statement."

As James Wallace wrote the jury's official verdict down on paper, John Hight grabbed his own paper and began scribbling his objections to the findings.

Wallace cracked open the jury room door and spotted the mayor. As formal as he could Wallace said, "Mr. Mayor, we have reached a verdict." It had taken less than two hours for a decision to be reached. It was late in the afternoon of the second day of the inquest, and the gallery spectators were still milling around outside the courthouse.

"This hearing is back in session," Mosby loudly proclaimed, as he slammed his gavel down on the judge's bench. It wasn't long before the gallery was filled up again. "Has the jury reached a verdict in this case?"

"We have," replied Wallace. The jurors had taken their place in the jury box once again.

"Please tell the court what you've found."

Wallace stood and unfolded a paper from his pocket. He cleared his throat.

"We the jury find that the Reverend Nathan Sweatt came to his death by the hands of some party or parties unknown to the jury and that his death was brought about by hanging by the neck, after which his body was thrown into the stream."

Mosby looked at the jurors. "So say you all?"

"No," Wallace said. "We have a dissenting opinion." Mosby looked at the gallery, then back at the jurors, wondering which of the six it could be. "He would like to read a statement," added Wallace.

"Well, go on then," Mosby prodded.

As James Wallace took his seat John Hight stood and faced the judge's bench. He held a piece of foolscap in his hand. He began to read from his notes.

"If it please the court," Hight began, "I don't believe sufficient effort has been made to discover the guilty parties." He paused for effect. "And furthermore, I think every soldier in the command, with the officers, and also the commander of the post, ought to be placed under arrest and held for their appearance before the next circuit court to answer for their crime." John Hight refolded his paper. "There ya have it," he said, and sat back down.

Massey and Burke shifted uneasily in their seats as those in the gallery behind them began talking loudly among themselves. This was the first time the five other jurors had heard what Hight had written.

While the commotion in the courtroom continued, Jim Wallace sat thinking about Hight's statement. Yes, he thought to himself, that would be the logical thing to do in normal times. Arrest the command, the soldiers, and charge them in civil court. But these weren't normal times. We're in a war. We have no authority over the military. They would resist. The citizens here, for the most part, lack arms and ammunition, and that's the way the matter would end. No, John Hight was climbing up the wrong tree.

Mosby banged his gavel hard on the bench. "Please, let's have some order here." He almost had to yell this. Then, looking at Hight, he said, "I don't think that's practical, Mr. Hight. But this court acknowledges your dissenting vote. Thank you. This court hereby accepts the verdict of the jury and is now dismissed. This inquest is completed and the hearing over."

The following Sunday the Reverend Sweatt's congregation once again gathered in the small clapboard church in Liberty Chapel. Margaret Sweatt sat in the first row with her children, as she always did. Albert and Sally Mitchell sat to one side of her. The three held hands as everyone in the meeting hall burst forth with *A Mighty Fortress Is Our God*. Tears flowed down Margaret's cheeks as she sang, "And though this world, with devils filled, should threaten to undo us, we will not fear, for God hath willed his truth to triumph through us."

When the hymn ended Albert Mitchell stood and walked to the pulpit. He had rehearsed, with Margaret's help, what he would read from the Bible. He knew what to say and how to say it. In a strong clear voice the stooped old man leaned forward and, holding the book, read, "Dearly beloved, avenge not yourselves, but rather give place unto wrath: for it is written, Vengeance is mine; I will repay, saith the Lord. Therefore if thine enemy hungers, feed him; if he thirsts, give him drink: for in doing so thou shalt heap coals of fire on his head."

There was a new face in the congregation that Sunday. A young soldier in a baggy, ill-fitting uniform sat in the back of the church. His hat lay in his lap. It was Thomas, the orderly who had brought Nathan Sweatt his food in the guardhouse. He had come to hear what it was all about.

# 13

# The Epilogue

No one was ever charged with the murder of the Reverend Nathan Sweatt. Captain Massey steadfastly maintained his innocence in the entire affair. James Wallace, the Chancery Clerk of Attala County, would write years later "...that it is doing but an act of justice to Capt. Massey to say that he always denied having any knowledge of, or in any way abetting in the murder, affirming that he really had ordered soldiers to carry Mr. Sweatt to headquarters and supposed they had done so until his body was found..." And that this "...caused him great surprise, and he believed that soldiers, thirsting for revenge for the firing upon them and wounding of their comrades, had, under cover of carrying him to headquarters, and having his person in charge, proceeded to satisfy their revenge by murdering him."

Massey's men were not mustered from Attala County. The soldiers were not familiar with the countryside. To travel in darkness of night through woods and swamps, to that particular spot on the Yackanookany River would have required the help of a local guide who knew the way well. No one was ever held to answer that point.

Conrad Massey was killed at Pine Mountain, Georgia, in February 1864. He was a major at that time.

The only invasion of Attala County by Union forces came on February 24, 1864. It took the Yankee column 38 minutes to pass through Kosciusko, having entered the town at about nine in the morning. A few soldiers raided the town stables looking for horses, and one broke through the courthouse doors. James Wallace had removed the county records and papers the day before and had taken them four miles northwest out of town, hiding them in a farmer's loft. The only item removed from the courthouse was the seal of the Chancery Court. Wallace had inadvertently left it on the mantle over the fireplace.

On Sunday, June 5, 1864, a funeral service was preached for Reverend Sweatt.

When Robert E. Lee surrendered in 1865 the large stores of food in Kosciusko which Captain Parr, Massey's commissary officer, sat on during the war were eventually broken open by the town's citizens and distributed to widows, orphans, and the destitute. Those who lived further out in the county, away from town, were not so lucky, as transportation of the supplies proved impracticable. The distribution needed to be done hastily. There was the possibility that the stores might be stolen by raiders from the north county. They were still roaming the countryside even at the war's end.

The Attala County courthouse in which Reverend Sweatt was held prisoner was destroyed by fire in the early morning hours of July 26, 1896. The current courthouse opened in 1897.

Attala County was formed in 1833, fifteen years before Nathan Sweatt brought his family to Mississippi. Kosciusko, the county seat, was named in honor of Tadeusz Kosiusko, the Polish general and engineer who fought in the American Revolutionary War. He helped fortify Fort West Point in 1778. Kosciusko was originally named Red Bud Springs for a natural spring that was present in the town. The name was changed to Kosciusko in 1837. Local folklore and family tradition has referred to the Deep Hole as "Sweatt's Hole."

William Thomas Sweatt, the Reverend's oldest son, remained in the Indian Territory, where he died November 18, 1911. He is buried in Maple Grove Cemetery, Seminole County, Oklahoma.

Nathan Nawls Sweatt, William's younger brother, would eventually return to Attala County from the Indian Territory. He and his wife, Sarah Bridges, would have eight children, one of whom, Cornelius Theodore (C.T. or Theo, as he was called), is the author's grandfather. Nathan Nawls died July 11, 1904, and is buried near his father.

Margaret Sweatt, the Reverend's wife, lived the rest of her life in Attala County. The 1880 county census lists her as being 65 years old. She is buried next to her husband in the Liberty Chapel Cemetery.

Nathan Sweatt is buried in Liberty Chapel Cemetery, Ethel, Mississippi. The Reverend's headstone reads:

"I am he that liveth, and was dead,
And behold I am alive for evermore."
Rev. N. Sweatt
Died
October 6, 1863
Aged 56 Years
"Remember me as you pass by.
As you are now so once was I
As I am now, so you must be,
Prepare for death and follow me."

# Bibliography

*Civil War Times Illustrated*: October 1982, Volume XXL, Number 6.

Coggins, Jack. *Arms and Equipment of the Civil War*. New York: Doubleday, 1962.

Kosciusko-Attala Historical Society. *Kosciusko-Attala History*. Marceline, MO: Wadsworth Publishing Company, 1976.

Niles, Jason (1814–1894). *Diary of Jason Niles, June 22, 1861–December 31, 1864*

Prince, Tim. *Civil War News*. September 9, 2022.

Rigdon, John C. *Historical Sketch and Roster of the Mississippi 20th Infantry Regiment*. Mississippi Regimental Series, January 26, 2021.

Wallace, James H. *History of Kosciusko and Attala County*, 1916.

*War of the Rebellion: A Compilation of the Official Records of the Union And Confederate Armies*, 1880–1901.

*9 7 9 8 3 8 5 2 4 5 6 0 4*